was born at Ashfield, Sydney [...]
Frances and Oswald Holme Barn[...]
of Sydney, graduating in 1918 a[...]
but did not accept this when [...]
permission. She then took up librarianship, working at the Sydney
Teachers' Technical College, a job she found tiring and un-
stimulating. During the 1920s she continued to live quietly with
her parents.

Whilst attending the University, Marjorie Barnard met Flora
Eldershaw and they established a successful and productive literary
collaboration, writing as M. Barnard Eldershaw. This lasted until
Flora Eldershaw's death in 1957. Their first novel, *A House Is
Built* (1929), was awarded, with Katharine Susannah Prichard's
Coonardoo, the *Bulletin* prize for the best novel submitted in
1928. *Green Memory* followed in 1931. Four years later Marjorie
Barnard gave up her job to become a full-time writer, encouraged
and supported by her friend, the critic and literary journalist,
Nellie Palmer. She described herself as seeking 'some sort of
fulfilment, to run my vital energy into a creative mould instead of
just letting it soak into the thirsty sand of a daily round'. In the
same year Marjorie Barnard joined the Fellowship of Australian
writers, of which Flora Eldershaw was President. For the next five
years, they, together with the writer, Frank Davison, were to
enjoy the reputation as 'the triumvirate'. 1935 too, marked the
beginning of Marjorie Barnard's political involvement: although
she never joined any political party she was nevertheless affected
by the social and political upheavals of the 1930s. *The Glasshouse*
(1936) reflects this development, as does *Plaque of Laurel* (1937).
By now Marjorie Barnard and Flora Eldershaw had become
leading literary figures in Sydney. Their partnership extended
beyond the field of fiction: the published criticism, including
Essays in Australian Fiction (1938) and numerous biographical
and historical books. Of the source of this collaboration Marjorie
Barnard said, 'we used to talk about the books we would write,

and it occurred to us that it would be much more fun to write together'. She produced most of the creative writing, with Flora Eldershaw responsible for development and structure. Flora Eldershaw, in contrast, wrote most of their critical work, with Marjorie Barnard consulting.

The year 1940 saw dramatic changes in Marjorie Barnard's life; she became a pacifist, and her father died, leaving her alone with an ailing mother. In 1942 she returned to librarianship, also working on her collection of short stories, *The Persimmon Tree* (1943).

Tomorrow and Tomorrow and Tomorrow (1947), also published by Virago, represented a major break in Marjorie Barnard's writing, as well as the culmination of her political ideals throughout the 1930s. Written with Flora Eldershaw, this apocryphal novel took five years to produce and was only published after being severely cut by the government censor. Discouraged by this, Marjorie Barnard turned away from fiction, concentrating instead on history and criticism. However, *Tomorrow and Tomorrow and Tomorrow* belatedly received the acclaim it deserved: in 1983 Marjorie Barnard was the recipient of the Patrick White Award for the novel, which was described by the judging committee as a 'complex, highly original book . . . which deserved a high place in Australian literature'. In 1984 she was awarded a Special Medal – previously only awarded to Christina Stead – in the New South Wales Premier Awards, in recognition of her life and work.

Her other works are: for children, *The Ivory Gate* (1920), an historical monograph, *Macquarie's World* (1941); *Australian Outline* (1943); *A History of Australia* (1962); *Miles Franklin: A Biography* (1967) and, together with Flora Eldershaw: an historical monograph, *Phillip of Australia* (1938); *The Life and Times of Captain John Piper* (1939); and *My Australia* (1939).

Marjorie Barnard now lives at Point Clare, New South Wales.

VIRAGO
MODERN
CLASSIC

NUMBER

190

THE
PERSIMMON
TREE

AND OTHER STORIES

MARJORIE BARNARD

Published by VIRAGO PRESS Limited 1985
41 William IV Street, London WC2N 4DB

The Persimmon Tree and Other Stories first published by
The Clarendon Publishing Company, Sydney 1943
Copyright © Marjorie Barnard 1943

Speak To Me from *Coast to Coast*, Australian Stories first published by Angus and
Robertson Ltd., Sydney 1945
Copyright © Marjorie Barnard 1945

Tree Without Earth
Copyright © Marjorie Barnard 1985

One Bright Leaf first published in *Quadrant* 1982
Copyright © Marjorie Barnard 1982

British Cataloguing in Publication Data
Barnard, Marjorie
The persimmon tree and other stories. —
(Virago modern classics)
I. Title
823[F]   PR6003.A687

ISBN 0-86068-628-0

Printed in Great Britain by Cox and Wyman at Reading, Berkshire.

ACKNOWLEDGEMENTS

The Author wishes to thank : John Fairfax and Sons Pty. Ltd. for permission to reprint the following stories which appeared in *The Home* and *The Home Journal*. " Arrow of Mistletoe;" " The Persimmon Tree," " The Bride Elect," " Beauty is Strength," " Canaries Sometimes Advertise," " The Woman Who Did the Right Thing," " It Will Grow Anywhere," " The Wrong Hat," " Dialogue at the Ballet," " The New Dress," " Sunday," " Dry Spell."

The Editor of *The Bulletin* for permission to reprint " The Lottery."

The Editor of the *ABC Weekly* for permission to reprint " The Dressmaker " and " Fighting in Vienna."

Messrs. Angus & Robertson for permission to use again " Dry Spell " and " The Persimmon Tree " which appeared in *Coast to Coast*.

MARJORIE BARNARD.

CONTENTS

ARROW OF MISTLETOE

Because she loved him she knew when he was distressed, even when he had successfully hidden it from himself ; and because she had complete faith in him, sometimes she was afraid. She never made the least effort to understand his financial transactions, though he talked to her enough about them. His imagination—he was a man of creative imagination working in the financial field— drew stimulus from the lambent trust and love in her wide, hazel eyes. It led him on. He did things then and afterwards—but more particularly afterwards— that a man with a clever wife might not have done. She certainly reassured him on the point that most people were fools. She encouraged in him the streak of bravura which made him so spectacular a figure, by not recognising it as anything out of the way. All those companies and trusts and things were his toys. She never for a monemt imagined that they were real. She wanted him to be happy. Even being rich was a game she played to please him. There had been ups and downs, some of them very declivitous, and they had left their hidden mark on her. She had learnt to wince. She might be stupid . She was also sensitive. And she loved him. She trusted him.

She was in a way quite an asset. Some people, a few, thought it a curious aberation that a financial genius, like Gilespie Munro, should openly idolise this slender little thing with the heart-shaped face of a delicate child and the pretty manners of a well trained débutante.

Others found it touching. No breath of scandal ever connected his name with any other woman's. The idea got round that because he was faithful to his wife he was a decent sort of chap, and a man you could trust. Astute business men were influenced by the fact. Tough people are usually sentimental—the harder the head the softer the heart. It helped to build up confidence. Confidence was Gilespie Munro's raw material. Give him enough and he could build Xanadu overnight. He could do marvels with it, not because he was a swindler but because he was an artist. He believed—and he was long past believing in anything else—that the thing you imagined was as real as the thing you had, beside being much better in every other way. There were times in his career when he had walked the tight rope over chasms and even the tight rope and been imaginary. So far he had always reached the other side. It was a matter of faith, in himself and in others.

Widows thought he was Galahad. That wasn't the same thing, but it was profitable.

Lisca Munro played her part. She was, if in a rather original way, her husband's helpmate. She was part of his curious legend, for it was certainly bizarre for such a man to live in respectable felicity with his wife, and to exhibit to the world not diamonds round her neck but trust in her eyes.

A career like Gilespie Munro's cannot stand still, nor can it even move at a moderate pace. The big scale adventurer must amaze by his audacity, his intrepidity, his brilliance. His methods must conjure up the imagination of those he leads and lives upon, yet he must continually outstrip them. He must make them mad in his own likeness or there will be nothing on which to float his schemes, but, if they ever catch up to him he becomes a commonplace and so is ruined. Suspecting themselves they will see through him. He must keep them dazzled. He must increase his light till one day someone notices that the sun is a black spot beside it and then the word goes round that things are a little queer, not quite sound.

Just before the war Gilespie Munro reached a crisis in his affairs. The moment had come when he must transform confidence into faith, the most chancy of miracles and one that required all his flair, all the sublety of his most blatant bravura. To clinch his schemes—the most stupendous and far reaching his brain had ever conceived—he needed, not argument but some fabulous gesture.

The schemes themselves he had created largely in monologue with Lisca. Pacing up and down the great gallery of glass and steel overhanging the harbour, that gave to his home the quality of a luxury liner, he built up, elaborated, shaped and tested the Idea from its first conception in his fertile brain. Hour after hour, day after day, Lisca listened to him and gave him her attention. It was always like that. He could not, in his seasons of creativeness, work alone, or on paper. He must talk and intoxicate himself with talking ; he must have for his anvil the plasticity of another mind, any mind, but in practice it must be Lisca's because in all the world he only dared trust Lisca completely. She didn't understand, and even the chinks of her incomprehension were stopped with love. She had the best, the most serviceable kind of faith, the faith that did not even try to understand.

It was tiring for Lisca, but she was glad. It meant the breaking of the drought. Something like this was due and overdue. She knew, she had felt for some time, that things were going badly with them. There had been no change in the externals of their life, yet she had felt everywhere ebbing credit pull like a tide and, though he had never abated his sales talk, she had sensed distress and flagging in her husband. Now that was gone. They would climb again out of their trough. Gil would be happy and dynamic, and the tide of money would come pouring in again.

The Idea had taken shape before her eyes like a vast cumulus. Monopoly Mortgage. A Creditors' Combine. The compounding of securitites on the grand scale for fixed incomes, the piecing together from them of a far-reaching hold over industry, swamping of boards, control of banks through the massing of overdrafts till the financial system became the inevitable plaything of one overgrown debtor. Power treated like money, and money treated like power. Shareholders subscribing not money, but securitites. Power leased to politicians and interest collected in parliamentary, not treasury, bills.

Out of the fiery nebula something cold and implacable was eventually shaped. Gilespie Munro began to organise. Of course the law would have to be altered but that was not difficult if the right people were interested. Involve enough of the right people—the really powerful people—those with most to lose, and the scheme was safe. They would safeguard it as part of Their Order. They must protect themselves. The others, the share-holders, would be necessary padding. So Gilespie Munro sent out his bright young men to work every field, set up his screen of publicity, pursuaded men to work for him who had no idea they were working for him, alien-ated those whose hostility would be useful, sowed strange seed in many furrows, created a legend and wrote a prospectus. . . .

The Idea came back to him from a hundred sources. Monopoly Mortgage was in the air. It wore the face of Financial Salvation. It became the Investor's Dream. Gil had his mass backing. It remained only to storm the inner circle of half a dozen men, and of these only one or two mattered. Even in them the artist was hidden somewhere and so they were, or should be, susceptible to magic. One man in particular Gilespie Munro believed to be the key and pivot. If he were convinced, the rest would follow. To convince him he would sweep him off his feet by some unrelated and unexpected tactic. Gesture not argument.

And so Gilespie Munro planned, with the daring of simplicity, his fabulous dinner party. It was to be a display of power as surely as a Roman triumph. The hundred most powerful men in the city—and their wives —were to eat his salt. A hundred mugs. And what salt ! They could sprinkle gold dust on their food and it would be cheap. Everything about this dinner, but particularly its costliness, should amaze, dazzle and intoxicate.

He expounded all the details to Lisca with an enthusiasm that she did not find contagious. For the first time she was alarmed. This was something she understood. Millions would not have disturbed her, they would have floated serenely over her head, no more real than toy balloons, but this dinner was going to cost money, money you could see. She was appalled by the amount. She knew for a certain fact that they had not enough money, that this was a wild and desperate business. The precariousness of their world was first revealed to her in

this dinner party. Her heart sickened with fear, not
for herself but for Gil.

She protested hesitantly. " But, Gil, the money, We
can't possibly afford it."

He laughed at her childishness, her dear naïveté.

" Money isn't real, my dear, only thinking makes it so."

Lisca was not comforted. He took no notice. He
went on telling her and telling her all about it and it
grew in the telling. He pointed to one name on the list
of guests.

" That's the important man—the one we have to
dazzle."

Lisca shrank. She thought she would have to sit beside this man and be part of the dazzlement.

Gil reassured her. " Oh no, you go in with the
Cabinet Minister. This old fellow." He flipped another
name contemptously. " You don't treat really important people as if they were important. Let them
think that you don't know. He'll sit here." He pressed
his little finger on a carefully chosen spot on the plan.
" He will have the best view of everything and yet not
feel himself singled out,"

Lisca acquiesced, but her unhappiness grew. This
dinner would ruin them. She steeled her courage to go
through with it.

When the day came it found her adequate. The
Important Man bowing over her hand found her altogether
charming. In greeting scores of people she had kept her
sincerity. She wore only the subtlest touch of make up
and round her delicate throat only a single string of
pearls. Among the hundred bedizened women she was a
rarity.

The Important Man sat in his carefully chosen seat
and watched the spectale with interest. He ate the
stupendous food with amusement. He looked and he
listened and congratulated himself on being at the top
of his form. He decided that he was the only detached
person present, the only mind that retained its objectivity.
All the others, not excluding his host, had allowed themselves to be dazzled. The thought put him in a high
good temper. The whole thing plucked at his imagination
and indulgently he let it. Gilsepie Munro could organise
victory. He'd hand him that. He was a man who Brought
Things Off and wasn't that the whole secret ? Maybe he
had brought something new into the world of finance.
There wasn't much doubt about the cogency of the Idea
but would it work ? If it worked it succeeded. But was
there enough confidence in all the world to float it ? The
foods, the wines, the scents, the pageantry wrought upon
him. The man was a magicain. This thing was bizarre,
incredible but perfect. It was only a sample, of course . . .
He saw through it, naturally. Munro obviously intended
him to. . . . All these people dazzled silly by a spot of
display. A nice little allegory. Clever. He'd split the
difference between their credulity and his, shown him
how easy it was to move them, harness them up, these
important people. Between us, Munro and I could clean
up the lot. . . .

The Important Man looked about him. He had the
habit of weighing everything. As one man of imagination
trying out another he tested every detail for a flaw. In
every dish and under every table he looked for his host's
feet of clay and did not find them. He could not have
organised a great coup better himself. His glance returned to what he considered the crowning touch.

He saw the white face of Lisca Munro, her anguished eyes, her trembling lips.

He followed her gaze. Four waiters were ceremonially carrying in a magnificent set piece. Shoulder high, with slow pomp, as if it were the ark of the covenant, they bore a crowning edifice of spun sugar and ice, wonder of the pastry cook's art, miraculously surrounded by flames. The diners were all spellbound for a moment then started to clap with joy.

THE BRIDE ELECT

The afternoon of the first hot day of spring hung heavy
as a drop about to fall. There was a feeling of departure
in the air. "A last supperish sort of day," Myra thought.
From the sheds a quarter of a mile away where the
shearing would begin to-morrow there came a confused
clamour. Myra was not sufficiently used to country
noises to know if these were normal sounds or not. Jim
would cock his head and say " That sounds like Benny
with the tractor in the boundary paddock," and Thea
would answer critically " It sounds more like O'Sullivan
to me," when, probably, Myra could hear nothing at all.
This confused noise, like a cloud of dust shot through
with the sharp yapping of dogs, hung on the rim of the
golden afternoon like the faint blur of irritation that
had settled on Myra's happiness. It only seemed to
emphasise the quiet that hung over the homestead. A
plump black Orpington had found her way into the
garden and was scratching complacently among Thea's
seedlings. She was the only living creature that stirred
about the place. The maids had gone over to their own
quarters and wouldn't be back till Ruby came to get
the afternoon tea. All the life of the homestead had
drained down to the sheds. The kennels under the pepper
tree, where the dogs were tied, were empty. They had
gone out rabbiting with Benny. Laddie, the sheep dog,
who was never tied up, had followed Jim down to the
sheds.

Thea was somewhere about, Myra supposed, but she
did not want Thea. They had long ago run out of things
to talk about. They had nothing in common, except

Jim. Thea resented her, Myra knew. She did not think that she would make Jim a good wife. She hated her delicacy. And it was that that Jim loved, her exquisite fraility, her helplessness. Thea thought Jim ought to have a sensible wife. Of course Thea had been very kind to her in her brusque way—but you could hear everything in this shell of a wooden house. There was a fragment of conversation that stuck like a thorn in Myra's memory. Thea's voice saying, " You know it never does work. A city girl doesn't settle down happily in the country. And a delicate one—They never fit in," and then abruptly, irritably, as if pushing an irrelevancy out of her path, " Oh, I know she's lovely." It really didn't matter what Thea thought, for Thea would not be here when they were married. She had said in her forthright way, "I'll be off as soon as the honeymoon is over." Jim needn't feel unhappy about her. Something hardened and stiffened in Myra. Jim was a dear, big softie. He'd mumbled something about Thea loving the place, growing up there. Perhaps he hoped Myra would ask her to stay. *That* sort of thing never did work. Thea had married. She hadn't loved the place enough to stop her marrying away from it. She had a life of her own and two boys and a girl at boarding school. Let her go and live it. Thea wasn't Myra's idea of a poor, helpless, widow woman. Still, she would rather Thea had liked her. She was Jim's sister. Everyone liked her except Thea and Laddie.

How the afternoon dragged on ! It was her last. To-morrow she would be gone. She could not help feeling a little aggrieved that Jim had left her alone this afternoon, and she had been irritated too by the way he had excused himself, anxious to point out how important his work was as if she might make a fuss like a child. It was the shearing, of course no one talked of anything else, the weather, the clip, the arrangements. It was all so *important*. It made her feel an outsider, as if she were wilfully being excluded. It made her even doubt if she were, after all, the pivot of Jim's life. Next year, when they were married, it would be her shearing too.

Myra was at a loose end. She wished now that she had asked Jim to get down her trunk so that she could pack. That trunk had been a surprise to Jim when it had been lugged out of the guard's van on to the siding. He'd whistled. Three suit cases and a trunk. He must have expected her to travel with just a bluey. He'd had to send the utility truck in for the luggage. But he had liked the frocks that came out of it. Her pretty things were always a lovely, exciting mystery to him. If only she had the trunk down now she could pack. Jim had swung it up there on the top of the wardrobe to be out of the way. It didn't seem to weigh anything in his hands, but, if she were to try to pull it down herself, she'd have an heart attack. She loved Jim's strength, it was like a strong wall about her. And Jim loved her weakness. Jim was going to make her really safe at last.

Myra moved idly out on to the verandah. The commotion down at the sheds irked her. It had only been going on for a few minutes, but it seemed to have been hammering at her nerves for hours. It sounded ominous, urgent, as if something was happening. Myra hated any sort of violence. It shivered and scattered the delicate world that she collected about her and that she needed. Thea belonged in that rough alien world, she could always turn out in an emergency and help the men. She always knew what to do, she had a whole world of values that were Greek to Myra. She had let her skin become weathered and her hands coursened, and yet somehow

everyone valued Thea. She made it quite clear to Myra
that she was an outsider but no one seemed to notice
her rudeness, not even Jim.   Thea had them bluffed.
Myra knew that Thea was unassailable, that while Thea
was there, she too would have to subscribe to this legend
of her being wonderful, or be accused of feminine jealousy.
What about Thea's feminine jealousy ? It was so obvious
that Myra could have laughed. But Thea was going
away. It was Jim's world too, but Jim wore it with a
sort of flourish. He brought it to her and laid it at her
feet. It was, in some odd way, Laddie's world more
than anyone's. Laddie, like Thea, did not want or trust
Myra, and Myra minded Laddie's polite hostility more
than Thea's. Laddie really was unassailable. Jim valued
him more, Myra thought, than it was reasonable to value
a dog. He was a Scotch Collie with lion coloured head
and paws, a darker back and great plumy tail, not a big
dog, getting old, and very gentle. He had beautiful
manners, and was a good sheep dog. He would only
work for Jim, no one else had ever handled him. Myra
wanted to be friends with Laddie, he seemed an easy
conquest. He stood politely still when she patted him,
rolling up his eyes at Jim as much as to say, "Is this
alright ?" When she had offered him food from her plate
the table he had refused it, turning away his head. She had
felt rebuked. There had been an odd little smile on
Thea's face. Laddie wouldn't go with her down through
the orchard to fetch the mail. " He never follows anyone
but me," Jim had explained. " He's a one man dog.
All good sheep dogs are." Jim hadn't tried to help her,
he hadn't ordered Laddie to go with her. He had in a
way taken Laddie's side.

She had even, just as if she were currying favour with
the dog, taken his side against Jim when she thought

Jim harsh with him. " He's a working dog," Jim
had explained, " you mustn't spoil him." There even
was something sacrosanct about sheep dogs, something
that she, an outsider, must not tamper with.

Myra leaned on the verandah rail and looked over the
country. It was beautiful and she loved it. It was wide
and gentle and good. She knew that she was going to be
happy here, it soothed her at once. The house stood on
a hill facing east, it was surrounded by a half circle of
wattles, tarnished now to bronze, but the view in front
was left clear. The garden sloped down into the neglected
orchard, the almond trees were in leaf, the peaches and
the plums in bloom, the wedge of vineyard, without a
single bud, looked blue. Beyond was rising ground
again, patched with the red of fallow, the bright green of
young wheat, and neutral sheep-coloured paddocks,
tussocky so that even in the distance they had texture.
(She must learn to hate No. 10 wire grass.) Beyond
again were brown-green hills on which a scattering of
trees showed like blue pom-poms. Here and there was a
silvery patch of water, a dam, and the big white silos by
the siding looked like a chateau. Myra knew that nobody
saw this scene with quite her eyes. It meant something
different to her. She knew it, coming fresh to it, in a
way they did not. And it flattered her, this big fertile
countryside. It made her feel like a changeling, a fairy
child.

Jim had been so anxious for her to like it, so eager for
it to please her. " It's not always like this," he warned
her. In the summer it was burnt brown—a brown purple
like the Arizona desert, she thought, never having seen
the Arizona desert. There were dust storms and heat.
Well, if it were too bad she could not stand it. Jim

would have to send her to the coast for her health. She couldn't stand much, so she didn't have to.

The noise had died down but it still, to Myra's sensitive perceptions, seemed to leave a bruise on the air. She walked through the quiet house. Someone was running up from the sheds. It was Jim. She saw with horror that his arms and hands were wet with blood. She went towards him. " Jim, dear——" He didn't seem to see her, almost pushed her aside. " Thea," he called. " Thea." Thea came quickly out of her room carrying a bottle and a roll of linen. " I heard," she said, " I was just coming."

" It's Laddie. The shearers' dogs got him, the whole pack on him."

They hurried away together. Myra could not feel even an echo of their consternation. She stood alone in the sickly quiet. She felt angry, baffled, despoiled. She went to her room, brought a chair to the wardrobe and, climbing upon it, began to pull and drag at her trunk.

Jim knelt beside her holding her head on his knees. Thea was pouring a teaspoonful of brandy, from the bottle she had carried down to the sheds, between Myra's blue lips. With difficulty she raised her heavy lids and looked at Jim. He was almost distracted with anxiety, but now it was all for her. She tried to speak, he bent close to hear. " Laddie ?" she asked.

" Hush, darling, don't try to talk." But the question in her eyes was insistent. " We couldn't do anything for poor old Laddie," he told her.

She let her lids fall. The tears trickled down her white cheeks from under them.

" Don't cry, darling," he pleaded in an agonised voice, " Laddie was only a dog."

THE PERSIMMON TREE

I saw the spring come once and I won't forget it. Only once. I had been ill all the winter and I was recovering. There was no more pain, no more treatments or visits to the doctor. The face that looked back at me from my old silver mirror was the face of a woman who had escaped. I had only to build up my strength. For that I wanted to be alone, an old and natural impulse. I had been out of things for quite a long time and the effort of returning was still too great. My mind was transparent and as tender as new skin. Everything that happened, even the commonest things, seemed to be happening for the first time, and had a delicate hollow ring like music played in an empty auditorium.

I took a flat in a quiet, blind street, lined with English trees. It was one large room, high ceilinged with pale walls, chaste as a cell in a honey comb, and furnished with the passionless, standardised grace of a fashionable interior decorator. It had the afternoon sun which I prefer because I like my mornings shadowy and cool, the relaxed end of the night prolonged as far as possible. When I arrived the trees were bare and still against the lilac dusk. There was a block of flats opposite, discreet, well tended, with a wide entrance. At night it lifted its oblongs of rose and golden light far up into the sky. One of its windows was immediately opposite mine. I noticed that it was always shut against the air. The street was wide but because it was so quiet the window seemed near. I was glad to see it always shut because I spend a good deal of time at my window and it was the only one that might have overlooked me and flawed my privacy.

I liked the room from the first. It was a shell that
fitted without touching me. The afternoon sun threw
the shadow of a tree on my light wall and it was in the
shadow that I first noticed that the bare twigs were
beginning to swell with buds. A water colour, pretty
and innocuous, hung on that wall. One day I asked the
silent woman who serviced me to take it down. After
that the shadow of the tree had the wall to itself and
I felt cleared and tranquil as if I had expelled the last
fragment of grit from my mind.

I grew familiar with all the people in the street. They
came and went with a surprising regularity and they all,
somehow, seemed to be cut to a very correct pattern.
They were part of the mise en scene, hardly real at all
and I never felt the faintest desire to become acquainted
with any of them. There was one woman I noticed,
about my own age. She lived over the way. She had
been beautiful I thought, and was still handsome with a
fine tall figure. She always wore dark clothes, tailor made,
and there was reserve in her every movement. Coming
and going she was always alone, but you felt that that
was by her own choice, that everything she did was by her
own steady choice. She walked up the steps so firmly,
and vanished so resolutely into the discreet muteness of
the building opposite, that I felt a faint, a very faint,
envy of anyone who appeared to have her life so perfectly under control.

There was a day much warmer than anything we had
had, a still, warm, milky day. I saw as soon as I got up
that the window opposite was open a few inches, 'Spring
comes even to the careful heart,' I thought. And the
next morning not only was the window open but there
was a row of persimmons set out carefully and precisely
on the sill, to ripen in the sun. Shaped like a young

woman's breasts their deep, rich, golden-orange colour, seemed just the highlight that the morning's spring tranquillity needed. It was almost a shock to me to see them there. I remembered at home when I was a child there was a grove of persimmon trees down one side of the house. In the autumn they had blazed deep red, taking your breath away. They cast a rosy light into rooms on that side of the house as if a fire were burning outside. Then the leaves fell and left the pointed dark gold fruit clinging to the bare branches. They never lost their strangeness— magical, Hesperidean trees. When I saw the Fire Bird danced my heart moved painfully because I remembered the persimmon trees in the early morning against the dark windbreak of the loquats. Why did I always think of autumn in springtime ?

Persimmons belong to autumn and this was spring. I went to the window to look again. Yes, they were there, they were real. I had not imagined them, autumn fruit warming to a ripe transparency in the spring sunshine. They must have come, expensively packed in sawdust, from California or have lain all winter in storage. Fruit out of season.

It was later in the day when the sun had left the sill that I saw the window opened and a hand come out to gather the persimmons. I saw a woman's figure against the curtains. *She* lived there. It was her window opposite mine.

Often now the window was open. That in itself was like the breaking of a bud. A bowl of thick cream pottery, shaped like a boat, appeared on the sill. It was planted, I think, with bulbs. She used to water it with one of those tiny, long-spouted, hand-painted cans that you use for refilling vases, and I saw her gingerly loosening the earth with a silver table fork. She didn't look up or across the street. Not once.

Sometimes on my leisurely walks I passed her in the street. I knew her quite well now, the texture of her skin, her hands, the set of her clothes, her movements. The way you know people when you are sure you will never be put to the test of speaking to them. I could have found out her name quite easily. I had only to walk into the vestibule of her block and read it in the list of tenants, or consult the visiting card on her door. I never did.

She was a lonely woman and so was I. That was a barrier, not a link. Lonely women have something to guard. I was not exactly lonely. I had stood my life on a shelf, that was all. I could have had a dozen friends round me all day long. But there wasn't a friend that I loved and trusted above all the others, no lover, secret or declared. She had, I suppose, some nutrient hinterland on which she drew.

The bulbs in her bowl were shooting. I could see the pale new-green spears standing out of the dark loam. I was quite interested in them, wondered what they would be. I expected tulips, I don't know why. Her window was open all day long now, very fine thin curtains hung in front of it and these were never parted. Sometimes they moved but it was only in the breeze.

The trees in the street showed green now. thick with budded leaves. The shadow pattern on my wall was intricate and rich. It was no longer an austere winter pattern as it had been at first. Even the movement of the branches in the wind seemed different. I used to lie looking at the shadow when I rested in the afternoon. I was always tired then and so more permeable to impressions. I'd think about the buds. how pale and tender they were, but how implacable. The way an unborn child is implacable. If man's world were in ashes the spring would still come. I watched the moving pattern and my heart stirred with it in frail, half-sweet melancholy.

One afternoon I looked out instead of in. It was growing late and the sun would soon be gone, but it was warm. There was gold dust in the air, the sunlight had thickened. The shadows of trees and buildings fell, as they sometimes do on a fortunate day, with dramatic grace. *She* was standing there just behind the curtains, in a long dark wrap, as if she had come from her bath and was going to dress, early, for the evening. She stood so long and so still, staring out,—at the budding trees, I thought—that tension began to accumulate in my mind. My blood ticked like a clock. Very slowly she raised her arms and the gown fell from her. She stood there naked, behind the veil of the curtains, the scarcely distinguishable but unmistakeable form of a woman whose face was in shadow.

I turned away. The shadow of the burgeoning bough was on the white wall. I thought my heart would break.

BEAUTY IS STRENGTH

She was a quarter of an hour late. She said haughtily, " I have an appointment. Mrs. Cedric Berrington." The girl's smile was as mechanical as the waves in her silver gilt hair. " Come this way, please, Madam."

The usual cubicle, cream matchboard walls, the basin with its barrage of taps and sprays, the big mirror, the sterilizing cabinet, not functioning, the chair, the penetential stool, the shelf with its powder streaked runner, bowl of clips, mat of invisible hairpins, row of friction perfumes, tattered copy of " Vogue." Over it a pall of soapy, steamy scent and the drone of a drier making the perpetual heavy summer afternoon of a hairdressing salon. Ida Barrington wondered how many permanent waves she had had. She felt that she had been in places like this far too often. A woman's age could be reckoned in perms. When you once began you couldn't stop.

She took off her hat and unscrewed her earrings. She needed this one. The wave was right out. The locks lay dank against her head. A sleepless night always took the life out of her hair. It was part of the weariness of being over forty that you daren't have any emotions, they took it out of your looks too much. A month at the beach hadn't done her hair any good either. It hadn't been a good holiday, too rackety, everyone being bright all the time. If the others kept it up you couldn't drop out. She would rather, after all, have stayed at home with Ced. When he had urged her to go she'd taken it for granted that he was being generous as he always was. What a fool she'd been. It put you at a disadvantage when your hair went phut.

Madamoiselle Paulette came in. She was petite, gamine, thirtyish, and had used her natural ugliness to the best possible advantage. They summed one another up instantly. Ida thought, " Not French, not Paulette, certainly not madamoiselle." Madamoiselle thought succinctly, " Wooden doll with the lacquer beginning to peel." These reflections in no way affected their intercourse. Women like this respect one another's bluff.

Madamoiselle prattled. She praised everything, especially her own services. " Yes, yes, of course, it needs it, but I can see just how it should be done. A big wave here, here, at the back tailored, and here a single row of sculptured curls. You see how it will be, so chic ? So sophisticated, no ? Madam is fortunate. The more fashionable the style the better it suits her. Madam has such a beautiful head, so small, so elegant. Madam will be entranced with what I do for her." It was the reassurance you bought in fashionable shops. Like a drug it began to take effect on Ida's sagging nerves. " Madam was recommended to come to me by a friend, is it not ?"

Ida said slowly, " Mrs. Bertie Chadwick is one of your customers."

" Ah yes, the so charming Mrs. Chadwick, so pretty, so sw-eet," Madamoiselle met eyes like swords in the mirror. She sighed. " If only Madam would use her influence. It is no pleasure at all to dress Mrs. Chadwick's hair. Those braids round the head. I ask you. They date. Really I am ashamed. It is so hausfrau." And she twisted her little pug face into a grimace that effectually drove out the golden image of Viola Chadwick.

" Alors "—Madamoiselle was gone and a silent girl in white instantly replaced her. Ida was led to the basin, shampooed, sprayed, dipped by strong mechanical hands, and returned dripping, swathed in a mackintosh cape and towels, to the chair in front of the mirror. Her hair black and spiky with water looked a depressing, meagre wisp. Her complexion had suffered radically from the steam. "What a hag," she thought. "Oh, what a hag."

The girl adjusted the drier like a high Egyptian helmet, laid the copy of "Vogue" in her lap, and departed briskly. Her hair stirred in the hot blast, the noise droned in her ears. The headache which she had beaten back with aspirin began again. There was a patch of wimpering nerves in her right temple the size of a penny and slowly spreading. But the worst thing was looking in the mirror. Her face suspended between the helmet and the mackintosh cape was just face, without aids or garnishings. It was from moments like these, when you saw your face isolated, that you learned the truth about it. Her mouth looked hard and disappointed, and round each corner there was clearly discernable, in this impartial light, a little bracket of wrinkle. You can't, she had read somewhere, do anything about wrinkles once they are visible to the naked eye. Her cheek bones looked high and stiff and on her throat, where age first shows itself, the working of the muscles showed too clearly, and the skin just under the chin was ever so slightly puckered.

The evidence in the mirror was germane to the weight on her mind. It was thus that she had always envisaged defeat, other women's, not her own. Cut off momentarily from everything except the mirror and the whirr of the drier, her mind was forced back again into last night's ditch. But now the pace was heavier. She was sure, with a leaden certainty, about Ced and Viola.

The shreds of evidence were working like splinters in her brain. There was the letter addressed to Ced lying on the table with the other mail when she came in yesterday afternoon. She recognised Viola's handwriting at once, large, eager, rather unformed. It didn't surprise her much, for Viola was in constant need of expression. She was for ever telephoning her friends about some new enthusiasm, writing little notes, copying sentiments that pleased her, out of the novels she read into arty leather note books. But this wasn't a little note. It was bulky ; even in Viola's sprawling script, a long letter. She had weighed it speculatively and put it by with an open mind. She wasn't, she often told people—particularly Ced— a jealous wife, nor would she be but for the possessive streak as strong in her as instinct in an animal.

She had gone through the house, the housemaid silent and insolently correct at her heels. In every room she stopped to alter something. It wasn't that the rooms had fallen away from the immaculate perfection that she demanded. It was there shining and clear, but everything was nevertheless different. She knew that at once. It was the only kind of sensitiveness she had. In a month the house had slipped away from her dominance whilst maintaining the form of her taste. No one else's taste had been substituted, it had merely been lived in by people who thought differently and felt differently from herself, and their indifferent hands had communicated this to every object of decoration or use that stood in it. This knowledge drew a web over her spirit. She would take the house back but, returning from that unsatisfactory holiday with her hair out of curl and her skin tarnished by the strong salt air, she had realised for the first time the burden these constant adjustments to the status quo could be. The thought, like a drop of water, had condensed in her mind, "From now on it will get harder and harder just to keep things as they are."

That hadn't anything to do with the letter. In fact, she had forgotten it until she found something else. But that wasn't anything in itself either. The laundry had come back and his clean clothes were lying on Ced's bed, not yet put away. Three dress shirts. And he'd said he'd been nowhere. He wasn't the sort of man to dress for his own edification. He always grumbled at getting into a boiled shirt but he looked his best in evening dress. How often the sight of his solid conventional grace had pleased her with its final rightness. To see those three new-laundered shirts was like picking up a bird's feather bright with the tell-tale mating colours. Had Betty seen it that way too, and was there a quickly, but not too quickly, concealed glint in her eye ?

At dinner she had asked Ced, as naturally she might : " What had Viola to say ?"

There had been an almost imperceptible pause. " Just a note to say that Bertie had to go to Melbourne and wouldn't be along for golf on Saturday and to ask when you'd be back."

" Why didn't she phone ?"

" How do I know ?" There was a trace of irritation under the casual words.

Ced was outwardly the same as ever but she was increasingly aware of a subtle change in him, like the one that she had felt in the house. The evening hung heavily between them, and when she went to her room there had been none of the rather apologetic overtures—more apologetic, less passionate with the years—she had expected. " I expect you're tired, my dear," he had said. " I'll say good-night."

Lying in bed, suspicion began to tick louder and louder in her brain. Her nerves at the moment were fertile soil for doubt. She couldn't relax, her eyes seemed to be held open by springs. Across the landing she heard Ced undressing and pottering about his room in a leisurely fashion. Presently he went into the bathroom, and she heard the water flowing. She hardly told herself what she was going to do as she crossed to his room. She hunted for the letter swiftly, thoroughly, silently. She even went through his suit encountering in all their innocency the personal oddments that fill a man's pockets. The letter was not there ; it was not in the room unless it was hidden in some fantastic place. She ran downstairs in her bare feet and hunted again in all the likely places without success. When she returned to her room the water was running out of the bath. She crept into bed humiliated by the blatant vulgarity of what she she had done. He had destroyed the letter or hidden it securely or—and fantastically this hurt her most—taken it into the bathroom with him.

Other thoughts began to assemble. Why exactly had Ced stayed behind when she went to the beach ? All she could remember was something vague about business. Why, for that matter, had they been seeing so much of the Chadwick's for the last year ? Bertie was dumb and played a shocking game, and she had never really liked Viola—she was too....too easy...so sweet, so indolent for all her eagerness, so romantic, so untidy in her mind, so quick to enthuse and forget.... She hadn't asked herself before why they went about with the Chadwick's. It must have been of somebody's volition, not hers. People weren't so important, just coloured counters in the game. It was the game that mattered, the complex game of fashionable living, that had to be played just right.

Viola and Bertie did the same things, knew the same
people as they did, they fitted into the pattern and one
had to have friends, so why not Viola and Bertie ? It
hadn't been more important than that till now.

Had this been going on for months ? Did everyone
know ? What an unutterable fool she must look.

A girl came in, switched off the drier and swung it
back. She pressed the palm of her hand to Ida's head.
" You're done," she said brightly. " Madamoiselle will
be along to wind you."

Ida's hair stood out in a bush, brittle and cantankerous.
Madamoiselle Paulette divided it and wound it strand by
strand on the curlers, tight against the head, and forced
under each, a circle of insulating felt. She prattled as
she worked and her small lively eyes were bright with
what may have been the accumulated triumph of seeing
other women perpetually at a disadvantage.

Ida's head grew heavy with metal, the curlers strained
painfully at the tender skin of her temples, lolling over
her forehead and beating, if she moved, against her ears.
She found Madamoiselle Paulette and her chatter intolerable. Why on earth had she come here ? She never went
to one hairdresser for long, for she was perpetually dis-
satisfied, and at present she hadn't one. This morning
when she had realised that the first thing she must do
to clear the decks for whatever action she was going to
take, was to have her hair waved, her mind had turned
to this place that Viola had recommended so eagerly. At
bottom it was a morbid impulse that had brought her
here. " A hair of the dog," she thought sardonically.
She was sorry. It was a vile place. She loathed it.

" You are winding them too tightly," she said irritably,
," it's hurting me much more than usual."

" You must suffer to be beautiful," replied Madamoiselle gaily and began to apply the soaked sachets.

Ida shut her eyes. Now Madamoiselle was connecting
the curlers to the machine above her head. This was the
worst part, the weight, the pulling, the heat, the suffo-
cating smell of the sachets. Her thoughts kept pushing
their way through the thicket of her discomfort.

What was she going to do ? And what would Ced do ?
No man was ever safe from making a fool of himself.
She could have taken a sophisticated view of the whole
thing if he'd picked up a little dancer, but this was different, a woman in their own circle, one of her friends. She
tried to move her head and was jerked into acute consciousness of her situation.

" Please, Madam, please," insisted Madamoiselle.

" It's burning."

" No, no."

" Yes, there." She wanted to scream.

Madamoiselle released two curls and fitted two more.
" I'll sue her if she burns my hair," Ida thought.

She stared at her grotesque image. There was a bright
red spot on either cheek. Her spirits plunged even lower.
She thought of Ced, her mind groping towards him, for
the first time in years, thought what he had given her.
She'd never imagined that he would let her down. When
they were first married she remembered that he had had
all sorts of romantic ideas but she believed that she had
cured them. They hadn't ever quarrelled, not ever.
Sometimes he irritated her when she felt that he was
begging her for something she didn't know how to give,
didn't possess. But she always bit her annoyance down.

She didn't for a minute believe that Ced had started
this. But that didn't help. What she was going to do ?
What if it were serious and he wanted her to divorce

him ? Her mind widened in horror. That would take
everything from her, her home, her background, her
position. A woman could only divorce successfully if
there was another man waiting for her. She would have
to make a new life. She was too tired, TOO OLD.

Like a little spark the idea began. She might forgive
him—the hardest way, without saying so. Just take no
notice. If she said nothing, did nothing, they couldn't
dislodge her, could they ? If anyone knew that she knew,
she would have to make a fuss and when she had made a
fuss Ced would be driven to some sort of action. If she
did nothing and let the thing wear itself out, then she
could keep everything or nearly everything. She had
reached her bedrock. Her dark circled eyes looked back
at her and she saw defeat in them.

The red eye of the waving machine glared down.

" We'll soon be finished," sang Madamoiselle.

Now the machine was switched off and the curls undone
one by one, relieving the pressure. Her head was covered
with small oily corkscrew curls.

" Divine," crooned Madamoiselle.

Competent hands shampooed her again and she felt
as if the energetic fingers must break through her tired
thin skull as if it were matchboard. Whilst she waited
for Madamoiselle to set her, a girl brought her a cup of
tea. They were tender with her after the ordeal. She
drank it gratefully and felt a little better. The sight of
Madamoiselle's deft fingers setting the waves reassured
her too. She did know her job and the wave wasn't
going to be a failure as she had feared. Already with the
hair fitted in a wet casque to her head she looked more
like herself. Half an hour in the drier and she would
be finished.

Yes, but what was she going to *do*. It had seemed settled a moment ago and she had determined to sacrifice herself. Now she was undecided again. If Bertie wasn't such a simp she could go to him and let him tackle the situation. The idea attracted her but she dismissed it. Bertie would just make a mess of it. How could Ced be so foolish ? She was pleased to find that she felt angry again—more angry and less defeated.

Viola wouldn't want a divorce, there were her children. Ced wouldn't want one either. Scandal would get him coming and going. They were, she supposed, just banking on her being a fool, and they didn't even trouble to take proper precautions against her finding out. That idea smouldered. The situation took on hard, new lines.

They released her from the drier. To the touch the hair seemed solid and caked. clogged as it was with fixative, but when Madamoiselle had combed and patted it, rewound the curls about her finger and burnished it with brilliantine, it looked soft and alive.

" Charming," cooed Madamoiselle passing her the hand mirror. For a moment Ida forgot her troubles. It was a beautiful wave, her head had never looked better. There wasn't a grey hair.

As soon as she was unswathed from the gingham cape, she began to make up her face, rediscovering all its lost virtues. She did it slowly, waving away the apprentice who obviously wanted to sweep up the litter on the floor. With delicate, skilled fingers she rubbed cream into her dried skin. She'd be a fool if she worried herself into wrinkles. The trouble would pass but the wrinkles would stay. She pencilled her brows and her whole face came into clearer definition. As she rouged her lips, she smiled. She wasn't so bad after all. There was plenty of fight in her still—and Ced wasn't going to get away with it. She, not he, was in the strong position. If he wanted to be a fool he'd have to pay for it. She'd punish him and then— she bent forward and looked into her own eyes, bright once more under the influence of eye shadow and mascara —and then she would win him back again. While she had her looks she could do anything. She had been through an ordeal but now she felt secure again. She wasn't even very angry. She had put on again the whole armour of sophistication. If anyone was going to look foolish it was Ced and Viola—especially Viola !

CANARIES SOMETIMES ADVERTISE

Spring was in the air.

The Managing Director, who prided himself on attending personally to every detail of the great store's organization, sent for the restaurant manager.

" I suppose," he said in a grudging voice, " that we'll have to redecorate the restaurant. Our public expects it."

The manager looked modestly down and murmered that we always did at this time of the year, didn't we ?

" Well," said the Director, " you'd better go ahead. Something original, something striking, something—er—"

" Smart ?" suggested the manager.

The Director frowned. " Not smart. It isn't going to be smart to be smart this season. No, no, something charming, a soupçon of sentiment," and he made a butterfly gesture, exotic in so stout a man, " perhaps rather amusing in an innocent way, but go easy on the sex appeal. You might even make it painlessly informative. Something that will please the ladies and advertise well. Take a turn round the show rooms and look at the new spring millinery."

The manager's dubious expression didn't come out of an American business manual, and it irritated the Director. " Jump to it, man, jump to it," and he added brusquely, " I've given you bushels of ideas. Keep the costs down and don't bother me any further."

The interview was over and the manager withdrew, his features composed as nearly as possible into the expression of a creative artist in the throes.

The great store kept faith with its public, punctually a week after the interview the restuarant was trans-

formed, practically overnight, from a Tudor Farm Kitchen
into a Woodland Bower, and all well-to-do citizens were
invited to eat Under the Greenwood Tree. Every column
became a tree with spreading three-ply foliage and giant
magnolia blooms; quaint animals from the toy department clung to the trunks and peered from the branches;
from every tree hung a bright brass cage containing a
very yellow live canary; the pay desks were transformed
into dove cotes; facsimile autumn leaves lay on the pale
green cloths artlessly advertising bargains in the shoe
department; on each menu was the picture of a feathered
songster with a short description of his habits written
by an ornithologist. The waitresses wore dirndals of
primrose yellow and green. It was everything the direc-
torate could ask—charming, romantic, amusing, informative, and novel.

The restaurant began to fill in earnest at twelve o'clock.
The ground swell of noise that takes possession of any
large restaurant at the peak hours had begun to gather—
footsteps, the scraping of chairs on parquet floors, many
conversations running together into one long murmur, the
fainter, clearer converse of china, glass and silver. On it like
flotsam floated the occasional cough or laugh, or, more
rarely, a child's crying. The tables were filling, vari-
coloured parterres under the trees. The waitresses were
unconsciously working faster and faster, keying up to
the daily rush, the nerve racking business of speed without hurry or disturbance. There was continual kaleido-
scopic movement. Clearing the murmurous noise by two
or three feet, the bird cages trembled a little in the warm,
gently moving air, and their occupants hopped restlessly
from perch to perch. Occasionally, one twittered or
essayed a few bars of song. Above them were the preter-
naturally still foliage, and the chandeliers glowing like

mutiple suns. Everything was strange to them except
the bars of their cages.

One of the birds, the plumpest, yellowest, most lively
of all the little cocks, had already had a couple of adven-
tures. He had flipped a sunflower seed into an important
cup of coffee, with the result that the owner had complained to the management, and he had so taken the
fancy of an old lady, used to behaving naturally under
all circumstances, that she had insisted on her grand-
daughter mounting a chair to feed him. He had not
taken any notice of the tomato sandwich that the embarrassed girl pushed through his bars, but he seemed
very alive to everything else about him. He hopped
from the perch to the floor of his cage, put his head on
one side, looked one way then the other, and hopped
back on to the perch. You would swear that he missed
nothing that went on at the four tables within his
immediate vision. His interest was pert and gay.

Three of the tables were occupied, the fourth was
reserved for the Managing Director who intended this
day to take pot luck with the public, a tribute to the
occasion. A waitress stood guard over it. "I'm sorry,
madam, this table is reserved." The raw seam of the new
uniform chafed the back of her neck, its colour tinted her
rosy skin with an unbecoming mauve. "There are two
good seats at the next table, sir. This table is reserved."
She hoped that no one was going to be disagreeable about
the table ; people often were, and the customer was
always right. So were the manager and the assistant
manageress and the superintendents. That left no one
to be in the wrong except the girls. And now they had
been dressed to match the canaries. What next ? It
could have been worse. They might have gone all Polyne-
sian and put them into grass skirts. Anyway, the canaries

were a change. She'd rather look at them than at people stuffing themselves. Poor little blighters, shut up in cages. I'll say they're quaint. Hopping round as fresh as paint taking everything in. But they'll get sick of it. What was that song—" She married the old man for his money and now she's a bird in a gilded cage "? Could do with a cage like that. It would be the great open spaces compared to earning your living as a waitress. Hope the O S's aren't going to make a set at this table. They're just the sort to remember the advt. " Free for all, no reservations."

The two large ladies and the thin little girl with the plaits moved in at the next table. They had large figures under iron control, large, thickly powdered faces, large jewellery, large handbags. They were alike because they thought about the same things and in the same way. But one had a stronger will which enabled her to do most of the talking.

" No, I haven't seen Mrs. Merton-Small for months. They lost their money. I told you, didn't I ? Yes, her husband never said a word. The first thing she knew a man came and cut off the telephone. She was as good as out of things then. I said, just as you might say, or any one else, 'Don't worry about the telephone, Mrs. Merton-Small, I've got one and you're welcome to come and use it just whenever you want to.' And, my dear, she did. She was always coming, even when Oscar was at home or when we were at dinner. Always in and out to that telephone, not to see us mind you, just to make a convenience of us." She deflected the stream for a moment. " Do you see the canaries, Margaret ? Aren't they sweet ?"

" Yes, Auntie."

" I thought you'd like it here. It's fun, isn't it ?"

" Yes, Auntie."

" There's nothing like it at home, is there ?"

" No, Auntie."

The little girl wished Auntie hadn't mentioned home. Once when she had been tiny she had been lost for half an hour in an amusement park, and though the details had long ago passed into a confused and hazy nightmare, the terror and strangeness of it was still lying just under the surface of her mind. It was much worse to be lost in an amusement park than anywhere else. It wasn't real, and because it wasn't real, anything at all might happen. She was always getting glimpses of it in tiny, terrifying peeps. This place was like it. And she felt lost all the time since. . . ' That's a canary, it's a sweet bird,' she said to herself. " I wish I had a canary."

" She had the most aggravating way of ringing up, if you know what I mean. Some people can make the simplest things aggravating, can't they ? She'd always begin by apologising for bothering us and I'd think 'If you know it's a nuisance, why do you do it ?' She'd never say who she wanted to telephone or anything like that, and she'd mutter into the telephone as if she thought we were spies. Oscar used to make a noise on purpose. He said I was too good natured. Perhaps I am. Anyhow, it dawned on Mrs. Metron-Small at last and she asked me did Oscar mind. What could I say ? I could only leave it to her good feeling. She got very red and said 'I always leave the twopence.' I really was angry then, Ella. Apparently she thought that because she paid twopence it wasn't a favour. She could just march in and out as if it were a telephone booth. Perhaps I shouldn't have said what I did. She didn't come again and now they have moved away. Eat your luncheon.

Margaret. What is the matter with you ? You are not going to cry, are you ?"

" No, Auntie." Though her mouth was still and her eyes dry, her face had the knobby and transparent look that goes before tears, and her aunt recognised it.

" Now, Margaret, be sensible. I came here solely for your sake, to give you a treat. Don't brood, look about you and enjoy yourself like a good girl."

The child gulped. A lump seemed to be forcing its way not through her throat but through her mind. The lump was always there, it didn't get smaller. If only she could cry it away. She pushed some food into her mouth.

" No, I'm not hard on her, Ella. It's terrible for a child to lose her mother, I know. But it's a month since it happened, and Margaret must pull herself together. She's not a baby, she's ten. It's no kindness to be soft with her. Fretting seems to have become a positive habit with her now. I really can't understand it, because Mary was just the gayest creature and you'd think her child..... Eat it up Margaret, there's a good child. Oscar said to me 'If people can't keep up it's just too bad, but you can't do anything about it. If they got ahead they wouldn't wait for you.' "

(The cutlet was made of wood. Auntie was made of wood like Mrs. Noah. She popped out at you. She wasn't real. Quick, quick, think of canaries.)

On the first Monday of every month they always had lunch together, the old man, very rich, stone deaf, his daughter, her husband and their little boy. In years the son-in-law hadn't got over the idea that he ought, by hook or by crook, to make conversation. The daughter knew that it wasn't necessary. She smiled and patted her father's arm. If the food was good she knew that he would be quite happy and satisfied just seeing them there. These occasions did not ruffle the junket smoothness of her mind. The little boy really enjoyed them. He liked seeing his grandfather eat. He recognised a maestro in the old gourmet, and although he was not a greedy child, he felt a deep satisfaction in this form of realism.

" How do you like the new decoration ?" the son-in-law began.

" How do you like the new decoration ?" the son-in-law began.

" Eh ?"

" Decoration. How do you like it ?"

" What's that ?"

" Birds."

" Eh ?"

" Birds."

" Oh, yes. Good suggestion. Spring chicken stuffed with truffles. Do you, young-fellow-me-lad ?"

The little boy nodded vigorously.

"Canaries," said the son-in-law in a semi-shout, pointing.

" Those. We'll have to pay for them but the food won't taste any better. Romans used to eat nightingales."

The child laughed out loud and his grandfather drew down his eyebrows in a mock scowl. The boy wriggled, laughing. The mother smiled. The taut and nervous son-in-law was the odd man out.

"Order something for me. Anything you think I'd like."

He choose the most expensive, the most exotic dish on the menu.

" Darling, I couldn't possibly eat that. You know I never eat things like that." She ordered for herself, competently, a pineapple salad. " You see you don't understand me at all."

He cursed himself for a clumsly brute. She smiled at him faintly, sadly, under the shadow of her black hat, big dark eyes in an exquisite pale face.

" Why did we come to this terrible, noisy place ?"

" You wanted to yesterday. You thought it would be amusing."

" I only said that because I was afraid of you. I knew if we went to a quiet place you'd start pestering me to be engaged." She drew off her long black gloves—she knew how to do it excitingly—and let her long, lanquid hands lie on the tablecloth.

" It's rather nice now we're here. Don't you think the canaries are jolly ? Look at that one !"

She shivered. " I don't like things in cages. All my life I've been afraid of the cage."

" Rosalie darling, is that why you won't be engaged ?"

" Yes, perhaps it is. Partly."

" But it's silly, sweetheart. If you're willing to marry me as soon as ever I can make you a home ,why won't you be engaged ?"

" I won't have a reserved notice stuck on me. It may be years before we can get married."

" I'd feel so much safer if you'd only wear a ring."

" I'd go mad feeling safe. I just couldn't bear it. I'm willing to trust you without any rings, or announcements, or anything."

" But, Rosalie sweet. . . ."

A middle aged lady and gentleman took the two vacant seats at the table. You could see at a glance that they were both fussy and devoted. The lovers exchanged eloquent looks, and fell silent. They had been enjoying themselves immensely.

The newcomers put their heads together over the menu.

" I really would like that," said the lady wistfully, her

finger hovering among the delectable viands, " but it
isn't in our diet, is it ?"

" No, my dear, but I think we might."

" Wouldn't it be rash ?"

" To-day is our anniversary."

" If you will, I will."

They smiled and sighed.

" What did I tell you ?" said Rosalie, looking wicked.
" I don't think, Don, that after all, I'll marry you at all."

It.was five minutes to one, and the Managing Director
had arrived with an important business friend, a mild,
frail old gentleman, so shrewd that you never suspected
it till several months after it was too late to do anything
about it. The plump canary had an instant succes with
him. He was, as he diffidently confessed, a bird fancier
in his scanty leisure. The canary chirped, hopping like a
grace note from perch to perch.

"Sweet, sweet," said the old man. They might have been
birds of a feather, the canary the more worldly of the two.

The orchestra had taken its place on the dais. The
burr of mingled and aglutinative sound in the great
restaurant had reached its height, a swell of sound with
a flying spume of light clatter.   Into it the music, loud
and compact, was launched like a ship. To the plump
canary it sounded a challenge. He lifted his head, his
throat swelled and he began to sing. The birds near him
were caught up in it, and presently all through the room
canaries were singing. They sang with all their might,
their hearts swelled to bursting, against the orchestra.
The volume mounted and mounted, eighty canaries
singing in a passion of competition.

All the human particles beneath the singing canopy
were swept together. The waitresses hurrying with their
loaded trays stood still, diners in the act of arriving or

departing were immobilised as if the air had hardened about them. Every head was raised. An elderly spinster who had just come out of a nerve hospital tried to start a revivalist meeting. The old business man closed his eyes and his face moulded into the still, beatific smile of the dead. The little girl, Margaret, suddenly pushed away her Neopolitan ice, and, pillowing her head on her arms, began to cry. The hard lump was melting and she could cry grief out of her breast without let or hindrance. The aunt took no notice. The little puce mouth in her big face was open and slack with amazement. Was this a stunt or had it just happened ? Don could feel Rosalie trembling from head to foot with a fine inner vibration. Slowly she turned her face towards him. The old married couple whose blood stream was purified by diet, held hands unashamedly. The deaf man stopped eating and stared about him in wonder. He certainly heard something, he wanted to know if it was the Communists.

The orchestra stopped playing, then one by one the canaries stopped singing. People sighed as if they were coming to from a faint, laughed foolishly, spoke loudly, began to move, to eat, to hurry. The spell was broken but on every mind, like the moisture from a burst bubble, there lingered a trace of mystery. It had lasted perhaps three minutes.

The Managing Director sent for the manager of the restaurant. He came wiping the sweat from his forehead, the backs of his hands.

" What did you pay for those canaries ?"

" They are hired, sir."

" Send them back at once."

" Yes, sir."

" Once," said the Managing Director, relaxing a little, " is a good advertisement, twice would be a scandal."

THE WOMAN WHO DID THE RIGHT THING

It was strange how Barbara kept thinking that she saw Murray Hart. There was a man in a grey suit now walking with a girl on the path at the far side of the lawn ; she had been sure, at the first glance, that it was Murray. Her heart had leaped painfully and she had had a queer, white feeling round her mouth. It was not Murray, not even like him, very much younger, but there was something in the way he turned to the girl beside him, eager, taut, absorbed. . . . She was aware of it even at this distance. This was like looking in a mirror, Barbara told herself painfully, only in reverse. It was like the image of a dream cast on her waiting mind. She was obsessed by these pictures of a happiness she knew to be impossible, out of her reach.

Barbara walked slowly, at the same pace as the two across the lawn. They carried their own world with them, she thought, they saw everything about them, if they looked at all, with eyes different from her's, even the sky and the trees were not the sky and trees that she saw. A raw light poured down from the cloudy sky and there was a malaise over the gardens. Trees and bushes shrank before the wind, turning up the dulled or silvery backs of their leaves ; the grass was already brownish after an early spell of hot weather ; in empty flower beds the earth was dry and grey, There was no colour under the pale sky. Barbara reflected that it might rain, that she had no umbrella and that these were her best clothes. Her hat would never be the same again if it got wet. But these were small inconsequent thoughts that blew across her mind like the few, low, fleecy clouds over the close packed rain clouds in the upper sky.

It was natural that she should think of Murray to-day for she was on her way to an afternoon party at Dora Murchison's Macquarie St. flat, and it was there, nine months ago, that she had met Murray for the first time. She was walking through the Botanic Gardens to kill time, she didn't want to be the first to arrive. She was aiming at the comfortable anonymous, moment when the room was half full, everybody talking. Parties were always rather a plunge for her, she went to so few. But she was determined now to accept any invitations that came her way, to go on exactly as usual, just as if she were dying, and determined to hide it. Actually she had not seen Murray for a fortnight. They had said, smiling, that they weren't going to be childish and avoid one another, they'd still be friends, now and forever. Murray wouldn't be at Dora's this afternoon, because it was going to be a purely feminine party. But it was something to be returning to a place where she had met him, for she half believed that she would pick up some infinitesimal trace of him there, and take ghostly comfort from it.

"I am like a young girl in love," she reproached herself. "I have no right to this," she told herself bitterly "I am old enough to know better." She was swept with nostalgia for youth when at least love was not ridiculous, when one had a right to grief, even to a broken heart. She told herself, driving in the statements like nails; "I am nearly forty, I am a widow, everything is over. Molly is my life. I have done the right thing for Murray. That is all that matters.

This thought so assailed her that she stopped on the path and stood staring at a great cactus plant, arrogant

and ugly, with grey green fleshy leaves and a long raking
florescence still in bud. She could no longer see the young
lovers, they had turned away into a side path, but she
did not miss them, her mind had entered its labyrinth.

Of one thing Barbara was sure, she knew Murray better
than anyone in the world knew him or ever had known
him. Better than his wife, Phoebe. She had met Phoebe
Hart once, a handsome, competent woman, who looked
as if she knew how to get her own way. She had been
faintly, ridiculously surprised that, with that name, she
hadn't two or three double chins. Phoebe cared nothing
for Murray's music. To her it was a job like other jobs,
and she reproached him because he did not make more
money. It was she who kept him chained to teaching,
fraying his spirit, giving up to " giggling girls, without
a note of music in them," the time he wanted for study
and composition. Murray was vulnerable. The least thing
tormented him. She had seen his pain reflected in his
difficult, tortured music that no one understood. He had
turned to her so naturally for peace. Their's had been
such a gentle friendship. Murray, for all his great gifts,
was so much simpler than anyone thought ; for all his
high strung, restless temperament, so much gentler.

When Gordon died young, Barbara thought her life,
except for Molly, was ended too. Five quiet, eventless,
not unhappy years fell away, and then came Murray and
a slow, mysterious blooming had begun in her again.
The past was lost, there was only Murray. They drew
nearer and nearer to love in a sort of charmed silence
that was broken at last by Murray's eager, ardent
pleading. Then she had had to think for them both,
but most for Murray. She had had to look forward
and see where this was leading them. Murray, because
of his great gifts, his music, was the important

one. She thought of Phoebe too, but only because of what she could do to Murray. They had quarrelled once, Murray had told her about it, not the cause, but the quarrel itself, in veiled, broken, phrases, how she had " known how to torture him," he had had to " climb down," been " beaten " and Phoebe had made the most of her advantage. Barbara had seen how the whole affair had lacerated him and left him unable to work for weeks. He had thrust this humiliation on her with a kind of proud perversity. She saw an infinity of pain in the episode. Phoebe wouldn't spare him now, and his fine drawn spirit couldn't stand it. There couldn't be any secrecy. Murray was transparent. She understood that. It was something to be reckoned with.

There would be a scandal, Phoebe would see to that. He would lose the pupils he hated but needed, he would be dragged down. It wasn't these external things that really mattered, it was the damage they would do to Murray. There was only one road to peace and safety for him, and that was through his music. She couldn't bring more trouble upon him, distract him further. He thought he would find peace with her but she knew better, she knew him so well. Only in cosmic things could his great heart find shelter. So she told him that they could only be friends, that they must stop growing fond of one another while there was still time. . . And he had, strangely and miraculously, believed the words that were so thin and cold in her mouth. Perhaps he was working now, and that was why she had not seen or heard from him, perhaps she had given him something to put into his music, something more than the fever and bitterness that had gone into it before.

Suddenly it seemed to Barbara that she had been walking in the Gardens for a very long time. She realised with something like panic that she was already late for her party. She almost turned back for the persistant wind had chilled her inside her clothes, and her courage was shrunken. But she knew that it was no good indulging herself like that.

. . . .

Dora Murchison's long room overlooking the Gardens and the harbour beyond seemed crowded with women. It was gay and shining and the still, warm, air smelt of perfume, flowers and cocktails. Barbara felt like a dove among parrakeets.

" Barbara darling, I began to be afraid you weren't coming." Dora, with her arm about Barbara's waist, led her among the guests. Affection wrapped her round. It was as if she, coming late, was the honoured guest. She had been to school with most of these women. They had gone on from the fashionable and expensive school to fashionable and expensive lives, and Barbara had dropped out, only holding, in Dora's friendship, a single thread of the old life. Now she made them all feel young again. She was so exactly as they remembered her. She reassured them. They loved her.

" How young Barbara looks," they sighed.

" That's because she leads a good life," said Dora, and everyone laughed. It was impossible to think of Barbara as being anything but good.

Every one talked, groups formed and broke, there was laughter and the tinkle of glass. Dora brought Barbara a cocktail. " This is called Angel's Milk," she said, and laughed. Barbara let herself be carried, lightly and gently, by the party. She had stopped thinking, and the Angel's Milk warmed her. Again and again she had to tell her little story. " My husband died five years ago."

" Only Molly." " I don't go any where much." " I'd love to come and see you." The person of whom she spoke seemed quite unreal. Her attention was arrested by a sudden reality.

Some one said : " Phoebe takes it too seriously. One shouldn't. It always happens, dosen't it ?"

" Poor Phoebe, she has had a good deal to put up with, one way and another. She has been waiting twenty years for Murray to settle down."

" She is beginning to show the wear and tear. He can stand the racket apparently, but she can't. For wear, give me an artistic temperament, they're toughest."

" He is very charming."

" But difficult," some one added.

" That's what they like."

" Do you remember Murray Hart ? You met him here before I went to England," Dora asked, drawing Barbara into the group.

" She's only twenty and one of his pupils, brilliant, I believe. They go everywhere together."

" Well, really, I didn't think Murray would descend to cradle snatching,"

" Don't begin pitying her. She can look after herself. It's Murray who'll need the prayers of the congregation."

" Poor Murray."

Every one laughed " Now you've given yourself away, Catherine. We always suspected. . . . "

" How long has it been going on ?"

" It has only just blown up apparently."

" When is Murray going to do something ? His music,

I mean. We've been expecting some magnum opus for years."

" Never, I think. He's the kind that promises and promises and goes through all the evolutions of a genius and in the end never does anything."

" Poor Murray."

" But he's so attractive."

"And a dear really—when he isn't making love."

Barbara got away from the party, somehow. Dora ran after her. " But you can't go like that, Babs. Besides, it's raining."

Barbara waved forlornly but finally as the lift carried her pale face out of sight. Dora returned slowly and thoughtfully to her party.

. . . .

The rain swirled down Macquarie Street, not heavy, but thick and feathery on the wind. Barbara was glad it was raining. She wanted to walk and walk. She turned to the right again into the Gardens. A delicate lustre of colour had come back to them. The trees were dark and bloomed with rain till they looked like trees in a Corot canvas. Seeing it, Barbara thought inconsequently. " Corot was in love with trees." The wet grass was more green than brown, the upturned earth dark with mois-ture. There was a good grateful smell of wet earth on the air.

Barbara followed one path after another. walking with short quick steps while her thoughts raced down their own dark channels and a slow black tide of bitter regret and disappointment welled up in her heart. " For nothing, for nothing," she said over and over again to herself. Now something had crumbled in her. She wanted love, not Murray, only love. She had thrown it away for nothing.

She saw, or thought she saw, the man in grey and the girl in blue, standing together very close and still under a tree with thick foliage, tented in by the rain. Perhaps she did not see them. It may have been an illusion, but an agony of rebellion shook her and tears began to mingle with the rain on her cheeks.

" My hat is ruined," She thought, " and I don't care." She could not imagine that she would ever want a hat again, or buy one or do any of the small commonplace, cheerful things of which her life had been made up.

IT WILL GROW ANYWHERE

The orchestra behind the potted palms played a valse de concert with passionless verve. They always began with it. It tightened the tension like a pair of pliers. No one listened, but the clamant music, with its clipped sensuality, affected them nevertheless, stirred inchoate images, mixed with their blood, and reflected itself again in the stubbed melodrama of raised voices, broken laughter and parade. It was one more roof upon their close, bright, ephemeral world. After the valse de concert there would be a pause, then a tango, a pause, a rhumba. . . The pauses were hollow and dramatic, filled with chatter and edged laughter.

The Thé Dansant at the Golf House—the limited liability company that looked like a club—was an institution. The people were always the same or looked the same. They all knew one another. They were all agreed, for a couple of hours, to accept the same mirage. Here the illusion lived, buoyed up like a balloon on the warm air, that every woman was beautiful and charming, and every man had a substantial bank balance—or at least a large overdraft. There was nothing here to prick it, from the fraternal manager-secretary to the great fan of blue-powdered lilies in the mock-baronial fireplace. It was the tribal cave.

There were men in plus fours, and girls in tweeds and bright pullovers—marigold, scarlet, emerald—straight from the links ; women in eye veils and silver fox capes who had driven over in their coupés ; a few very young girls still too inexpert to hide their innocent, awkward grace ; a scattering of avuncular men, the necessary padding. There was a scent of cigarettes and beeswax and coffee with an inner lining of something faintly astringent, like crushed green grass. The women passed in little puffs of warm purfume, of furs and powder. There was food, so much reduced and stylised as to be more a ritual than a nourishment or even a pleasure— acrid black coffee served with a bowl of airy whipped cream a la Floriani, pale scones leaking bright butter on the paper d'oyleys, over-dainty sandwiches drifted over with strands of limp lettuce like the conscientious hairs on a balding head, tiny cakes, varnished and mathematical, that only the adolescent were ever seen to eat. There was music. There was dancing that was like, not dancing itself but, in its more cogent moments, the shorthand symbols of dancing.

They sat at a table that was a little withdrawn by reason of being in a bay window. Behind them was the semicircle of glass and the view, over the shining beetle backs of parked cars, to the sea.

One was lean, middle aged, with worn temples. A man not given to questioning the world about him and never, perhaps, challenged by it, his courtesy as ingrained as his income, neither stupid nor insensitive. A solicitor in a sedate line of business. He had his own place, which was not avuncular, and knew everyone. His companion soon would. In the perfect mask of convential prosperity were set the bright, inquisitive eyes of a pug. His suppressed vivacity and robust omnivorousness acted as a peculiar stimulus to the other.

" Which is Mrs. Curtice ?"

" The plump little blonde with her back to the light. In mushroom pink. The second Mrs. Curtice."

" I suppose she's one of the people I'll meet ?"

" Yes, you'll meet Violet everywhere. That's Curtice with the red neck and sandy hair."

" Oh, I've known him for years, on and off. Used to box with him when we were youngsters. He was a bit of an athlete then, plenty of go, but nowhere special to go to. Popular sort of chap ?"

" Well liked. Everyone knows where they are with Ralph."

" And where's that ?"

" Nowhere in particular."

" He gets there just the same, I suppose, and no one knows why. I've watched him from a distance putting on the whole armour of success—golf, rotary, avoirdupois. Didn't know he'd married twice, though. How do these chaps do it ? No looks, no brains, not enough money to account for everything. You and I haven't managed to get one between us."

" In these parts no bachelor is ever despaired of. Ralph's a pretty warm man now."

" The present lady looks well entrenched."

" She is. Everyone has forgotten Struan, especially Violet. She went out like a match six years ago."

" Death or divorce ?"

" Divorce."

" What was their trouble, or was it the same old thing ?"

" It was the same old thing, but there were complications. You see Struan was the perfect wife."

" Some of them do try that. It's always fatal."

" Struan didn't try. She was the perfect wife."

" How perfect ?"

" Perfect."

" You mean, she ran his home like a clockwork palace?"

" She did, but there was a lot more than that. You see, she understood him."

" Once a woman understands a man, the poor devil hasn't a rag of privacy left."

" It wasn't like that at all."

" Sorry, old man. She got a raw deal, didn't she ?"

" It should have worked out, but it didn't. Ralph— she called him Rafe—had a roving eye. It began to rove before they had been married a year. Struan didn't do a thing about it. After a while Ralph didn't even pay her the compliment of being careful. One evening I remember he was being a bit obvious. It was the first time, too, that I realised that Struan was different from the rest of them. I just thought of her as a girl who was getting hurt, and had it in my mind I'd like to knock the fellow down. Just as anyone might feel."

" Of course."

" Struan must have seen it in my eyes. She didn't say, as another girl might have, 'It isn't important,' only 'It's part of Rafe, you know. I can't pick and choose.' No cracking hardy. Just that. She had a rather shattering honesty towards herself as well as towards others. I think it might have been one of her difficulties."

" No doubt. That attitude works with a husband nine times out of ten—but not the tenth."

" Yes, Violet was the tenth."

" Was she dumb with love and all that ?"

" I don't know. I made a bad break once, after everything had blown up. I asked her if she still cared for Ralph. She gave me a startled look, and didn't answer."

" How long did it last ?"

" Five years, and I don't think anyone expected it to break up. Curtice was in clover. Struan had money of her own. I know she used to pay for her own clothes, never nagged him for anything. She gave him a background. The sort of thing other women tried to do with their houses and their parties, and couldn't."

" Did the other women like her ?"

" I don't think she was really popular, though they gushed over her a lot. I can't understand why. I never heard her say a spiteful thing about another woman. She was generous to a fault, and utterly loyal to Ralph."

" How did he stand up to all that perfection ?"

" I can't say he ever showed to much advantage."

" U-u-m."

" One takes sides. It's very foolish, of course, and the last thing Struan wanted. She couldn't bear anyone to sympathise, even when there was something obvious to sympathise with. She tried to have a baby, but something went wrong. Struan was so brave about it, Ralph didn't get a chance. I imagine she apologised for her incompetence. Felt she'd failed him, anyhow. After that she hardened up a bit. She used to talk the patter of the moment, very bright and amusing, but I never got the impression that she was happy."

" Then the tenth woman came on the scene ?"

" Yes, Violet. I don't suppose Ralph was any more serious than he had been all the other times. He always had himself bluffed at first. But Violet was. She kept house for her father who was retired. Rather nondescript people. Nobody called, I fancy, or took any notice of them. You know how cliquey people are here. If you don't measure up you might as well be ten years dead. Damned cruel, of course, I didn't think of it at the time, but knowing Violet now, I can pretty well imagine what she felt then. She had social ambitions, wanted to escape out of her dreary little home, wanted to marry. It was a life and death matter. They probably came here to better her chances and no one noticed her existance. You can imagine what she was like six years ago, two stone lighter, not so guilefully babyish, and as ready to fight as any cornered animal. I don't know how Ralph met her, a pick-up at one remove probably. Anyhow, she struck a spark in him, the usual spark, and blew on it for all she was worth."

" They're alike. Don't you see it ? Soul mates, I shouldn't wonder. Damn funny."

" She put pressure on Ralph, till he asked Struan to release him. Struan went to see Violet, sure, bless her poor innocent heart, that a little straightforwardness between them would clear it up. It didn't. They say that when Struan caught sight of them both in a murky mirror in Violet's shabby little drawing room she exclaimed in her high clear voice : 'My dear, how absurd. You look like the wife and I look like the other woman, don't I ?' Violet treated her to a flood of Woolloomooloo. I can believe it of her but not before witnesses. Struan retreated. Honesty and sanity and humour were worse than useless, and she hadn't any other weapons. You see how innocent she was at heart ? She'd always had confidence in these things. Violet was implacable. She hated Struan far more than she loved Ralph, and Struan was no match for her. She offered to divorce Ralph, but Violet pointed out that she had no grounds. Violet was careful enough to keep her own position inviolable, and his previous rovings had been condoned. The danger of manufactured evidence and the slur she felt it would cast on her romance, as, with a tough woman's sentimentality, she called it, set Violet against any such plan. Struan offered to let Ralph divorce her for desertion. That takes three years and Violet knew well enough that three years would beat her if she had only beauty's hair to hold Ralph with. Of course Struan was in an impregnable position, she had only to do what she had done so often before, nothing. But she agreed to let him divorce her. The thing was so ugly, so amazing to her, that she had no will to fight. She came to me about it."

" Did you fix it up for her ?"

" No, I gave her some good advice and sent her away."

" Weren't you a bit of a fool ? I beg your pardon. It was your opportunity, wasn't it ? I mean, you might have done everything to spare her, when another man, the kind that usually takes these cases, would just shove things along anyhow."

" It would have been against my conscience, legal as well as personal."

" It went through, I suppose ?"

" Yes."

" How did the other women take it ?"

" They said 'Aren't men beasts ?' but they didn't go near Struan."

" I gather that the first Mrs. Curtice was very good looking ?"

" Struan would have been lovely if she hadn't been so damned fashionable. She wasn't satisfied unless everything looked as if it had been bought. That's all part of it, you know. She took things too seriously. All the shibboleths. She really believed in them. She thought a marriage could be made successful by observing all the rules. She was a civilized woman and that means she'd let go, slipped out of, that secret barbarian life that women lead. They knew it. She was an outcast. She had nothing to fall back on. When she failed, her whole scheme of things fell to pieces. It wasn't Ralph, it was the failure that broke her down."

" Couldn't she be happy with the right man ? Someone who understood her ?"

" Yes, if she would only let herself be. Someone who realised how sensative and innocent she is under it all. But the trouble is she can't get over it. She blames herself."

" You still see her then ?"

" Oh, yes, she comes into my office every now and then, looking as if she had everything under control. 'I suppose you couldn't take me to lunch,' she says, fastening her glove with an elegant. studied gesture like something learned from a book or a film. So vulnerable."

" So you take her to lunch ?"

" Yes, and we go over the whole affair. It does her good, I think. Relieves her. But the trouble is, that having given me her confidence is a good reason for not seeing me again for months. She's so vunerable, so sensitive, so gallant."

The inquisitive man felt uncomfortable. He didn't want to look at his companion. Some men went out and got drunk, some talked. Why me ? he thought. He'd been made a victim, a convenience. He was irritated. This wasn't tragic, it was comic. It wasn't even comic, it was futile.

Dusk clung like gauze to the sea and the waves left arabesques of shining foam on the empty beach. The grey-green hills of the deserted golf course rose and fell as gentle as breathing. The casuarinas traced their ancient pattern against the faint green twilight sky. The golf house, like a ship from an unknown barbarous port, lay stranded and blazing on the serenity of the night.

THE WRONG HAT

It looked a very expensive place, but Gwenda had said to come here. She wasn't even to think of money because they were giving her the hat, and they wanted it to be just exactly what she liked. This was the first time that she had been able to buy any hat that took her fancy without so much as looking at the price ticket. She was going to do the thing properly, she owed it to the children. It was more than a hat, Peter said, it was the Great Come Back.

This was a beautiful room, large, high-ceilinged and serene—the sort of room calculated to serve as a prefect background for smart women. It was a pleasure just to sit here high above the crowded streets, the sales, the bargains, the Friday specials, in perfect tranquility. It was at once so sedate and so reckless. She knew how utterly rash and vulnerable that pearl grey super carpet, fitted right up to the walls, was. Everything was silvery, oyster coloured walls, grey woodwork, limpid mirrors, grey velvet curtains framing, like two great pictures, the view across the park and St. Mary's Cathedral to the tumbled insurgent sky line of King's Cross and, to the left, a blue bay of the harbour.

Only half a dozen hats were in sight, poised on stands like young masts, elegent, immaculate, nonchalant. One of them in shiny black straw with a tiny crown and a big tilt was, she thought, the gayest, smartest hat that she had ever seen. No doubt it was what the social columns always referred to as an amusing hat. But when she had, very tentatively, indicated it the girl who was looking after her had smiled and shaken her head. " That's not quite Madam's style."

Such a nice girl, as friendly and helpful, despite the sophistication of her rosy nails and sculptured curls, as Gwenda would be. Not a bit like a shop girl anxious to sell, only anxious to please. This was, had she known it the final flower of the professional amateur. She had gone to the workroom now to bring a charming little model that had only just been created and never before shown.

The only blot in the room was her old hat. The children had been quite right. " Darling," Gwenda said, " You're not *old*. I'm going to make you have nice things now we can afford them." And Peter, roughly tender in the way that always flattered her so, had said " Snap out of it, my girl. We aren't going to let you settle down into a professional widow. If you only knew it, that hat you are wearing is nothing but a funk hole." She could see it now for what it was, the dowdy hat of a dingy woman. But she didn't have to be dingy. It was just a sort of habit that had crept on her. After the shock and misery of Jim's death she hadn't cared what she wore, so long as it was something plain and dark and cheap. Having gone into mourning she hadn't had the heart to come out of it, not even in six years. Now the children had taken a hand and announced a second spring. She realised that they were right.

She looked at herself critically in the mirror. She had to admit that she looked quite . . . pleasant. Grey hair and a few wrinkles, of course, but not so bad. The light was kind. Here she realised what good things life offered and she felt that she had had a narrow escape from throwing them away prematurely. Her heart was light.

Her eyes wandered lovingly to the smart little tilted hat. Why wasn't it her style ? She felt in her bones

that it was the very hat. There wouldn't be any harm
in trying it on whilst the girl was away. She picked it
up, it was as light as a feather and beautifully finished,
probably came from Paris or New York and cost a pretty
penny. You couldn't say it was too bright or juvenile.

Carefully, she pressed the front of the brim against her
forehead and fitted the ribbon bandeau over the back of
her head as she had seen the assistant do. Unconsciously
she imitated her almost caressing gesture. She looked in
the mirror. Horrified, she peered closer. A pain, sharper
than she had known for years, twisted her heart, a despair more sudden and complete than she had believed
possible, engulfed her. The hat was jaunty and young,
but the face beneath it was old and tired. The hat jeered.
It threw into pitiless relief every wrinkle and blemish.
It marked the collision of two worlds.

With trembling hands she took the hat off and returned
it to its stand. An assistant and another customer were
at the other end of the room, their backs turned. No
one had seen. She sat down again, staring blankly before
her. She had seen the image of her own death, and in this
one moment it struck more closely home than anything
that had ever happened to her. This had happened to
her, to no one else. The children would never understand. They would try to laugh her out of it. She couldn't
tell them. Oh, but she had seen it, seen it. The six years
of her widowhood had been quiet and safe. She hadn't
challenged time.

The girl stood beside her holding the new model, but
haggard eyes met the smiling ones in the glass. Slowly
she shook her head as the tears welled.

" No, my dear," she said, " I can't try it on. . . . It's
too late," and she groped blindly for her old hat, her
faithful friend.

TINKLING CYMBALS

CONVERSATION IN A BUFFET

It was the peak hour in the buffet. A ceaseless clang rose to the serene grey satin-wood ceiling from the long counters and the little pens along the wall. This buffet was one of those barnacles that cling to the outer edges of the gay world. It would have been a rather curious place if it were not so commonplace. It was made up of odds and ends from all over the world. The wooden pens had obviously evolved from high pews in old churches ; the chromium plating, the shining compact orderliness beneath the hubbub was of the hospitals ; the long counters were recently reminiscent of the bar ; the decor was that of the cinema, and harmlessly American. The waitresses were cheeky but pretty, and the clientele, consuming three-decker sandwiches, waffle steaks, omelets and draught beer in globular tankards, were the sons and daughters, secretaries and lady friends (taking the day off) of the older people dining more solemnly and expensively in the great hotel over their heads.

At this time, one o'clock on a Saturday, everything was submerged in noise, the genial clatter of one big party. The stout young man in the grey suit took no notice. He was very used to eating in such places. He was eating oysters now, lifting them tenderly one by one out of their shells, laving them in the sauce Mornay, and conveying them to his mouth. . . . He was pre-occupied but he was too naturally thrifty, to carefully aware of values, not to pay proper attention to his oysters. He didn't intend to waste them on himself. But to the waitress's efforts at conversation he remained impervious. He did not think that it would be becoming in him to-day. The seat beside him, on which rested his new grey hat, remained miraculously vacant until a voice said :

" Why didn't you tell me you owned the place, you old ruffian ?"

" 'lo Jimmy," he said, removing the headpiece resignedly.

Jimmy tucked his long legs under the counter and stowed his hat in one of the slots provided. He observed the oysters.

" You're doing yourself proud."

" Yes."

" Celebrating something ?"

" Not exactly."

" You're a close one, Bobby."

Bobby smiled complacently at the compliment. The waitress brought him roast beef accompanied by vegetables-in-season in a bird bath.

" I'm getting up my strength."

" Well, well. I think I'll have a three-decker, they mayn't be strengthening, but they are filling."

" I'm going to propose to a girl," said Bobby, with his mouth full.

" What ?"

" Marriage."

" Bully for you. Who's the girl ?"

" Elsa."

" Elsa ? I thought of asking her myself once."

" What happened ?"

" Nothing. I didn't ask her."

" Did you ever ask a girl ?" Jimmy was not above learning.

" Not when I was sober."

" Pity. It's a great feeling, you know."

" Do you think she'll have you ?"

" Just between you and me she's been keen on me for a long time."

" You're a clam. I didn't even know you were going round together."

" We haven't been. I've only just figured it out. You know me, Jimmy. When I make up my mind it stays put." He gave an unconscious imitation of Mussolini and speared another potato. " I'm dead serious," he said.

" I'm sure you are, old man."

" She hasn't just bowled me over, I've worked it all out. The man who isn't married is at a disadvantage in every way, socially and in business. Think of the benefit to my health alone in having regular meals and a quiet home life. I'll be able to do twice the work I do now. And I shouldn't wonder if Elsa wasn't a help to me even there. She has a good little head."

" And a dinky little curl beside her ear."

Bobby frowned. " So I thought I'd take the plunge."

" The snag is you've got to keep her."

" Two can live as cheaply as one."

Jimmy uttered a hollow laugh.

" You can laugh but it's true. I ran it all out with a pencil and paper. I don't suppose I'll be coming here much now," and he cast a elegiac glance round the busy scene.

" Love is enough," murmured Jimmy to the last fragment of his sandwhich.

" We'll be married almost at once. I don't mind giving you a tip. It's cheaper to be married than engaged. An engaged girl expects a devil of a lot."

" You're shrewd, Bobby."

Bobby looked at the menu. " I think I'll have something more." He was arming himself from within. He decided on a strawberry cream waffle.

" What a thing it is to be young," mumured Jimmy, contenting himself with a black coffee.

" Of course there is Elsa's side," said Bobby, expanding a little over his waffle. " Pretty tough for a woman to have to just sit and wait and perhaps the man never comes. Elsa's a grand little girl. I'd hate to see her —you know what I mean—left."

" She's a grand little girl but I can't see her being left in the lurch."

" You left her."

Jimmy wondered if he had better explain. He decided not to, things looked better as they were. He knocked cigarette ash into his saucer, looked up and there was Elsa coming towards them. He nudged Bobby.

" There she is."

Bobby looked up, and the strawberry impaled on his fork fell back into the cream with a soft plop, for Elsa was not alone. She clung possessively to the arm of her escort. She was in full war paint, and wore her most brilliant smile. She threw the two young men at the buffet a jaunty nod to divide between them.

CONVERSATION IN A TEA ROOM

The younger woman pulled off her gloves slowly, liberating a faint puff of powdery perfume. She had long, narrow nails, lacquered mother-of-pearl, and her narrow platinum wedding ring hid under other heavy rings heavy with diamonds. She looked abstractedly around the tea room. It was a cave of quiet high above the noisy street, its windows, elaborately draped, looked on to a blind brightness that did not penetrate the room. On each mock Jacobean table, covered with plate glass that gleamed faintly, giving to the light a pale watery quality, floated three daffodils in a black glass vase. The custom for the day had hardly began, the air was not yet defiled with cigarette smoke nor the quiet by the clatter of cutlery. A clean, matutinal smell of furniture polish, of flower stems and water, added to the cool content of the room.

She pulled in her attention slowly and with difficulty as if it were a fish on a line, and looked at last at her companion who was saying, " What are we having, Lois ?" They looked together at the yellow card that told them what they could have. Amy's hands were older, more heavily ringed, the nails dark red. They ordered hot buttered muffins, asparagus rolls, a plate of cakes and black coffee with cream.

" I don't have breakfast so I'm usually hungry about this time," Amy explained.

" I only have a squeezed grapefruit."

" Is it good ?"

" I don't know. I think I'll go back to the black coffee."

She saw herself sitting up in bed, pale with sleep, breakfasting on black coffee and a cigarette. She liked the picture for she felt it was delicately depraved and knew that it was very young of her to think so.

" Gladys Sheilds is on an all-cucumber diet. She says it's marvellous."

Lois made a little face.

" Yes," said Amy, decisively, " that's just what I say. What's the good of being thin if you are leathery?" She looked with dissatisfaction at her muffin ; it was not buttery enough. She was wondering too, why Lois had begged her, with such soft urgency, to meet her this morning. There was no urgency visible now, sleek little thing.

" I've just been to the hairdresser's. How do you think he has done me ?" Lois touched the triple row of mathematical golden curls under the brim of her black hat. She felt softly aware of herself in every movement.

" Your hair always looks perfect, dear, it's such a marvellous colour."

"Oh, do you think so ? I think it's terrible to have golden hair, nobody believes it's natural."

"Aren't women cats ?" said Amy, incontinently taking a mirror from her handbag and peering at herself between bites. " I can't understand it. Well, after all. . . Live and let live is my motto. Of course, a good hairdresser is terribly important."

" He's a Russian. He lost everything in the revolution. He didn't actually say so, but I gathered his father was someone very important. Just one or two things he let slip. He told me a lot about himself."

" That's funny."

" I'm not a snob. I mean we're all here in the world together, aren't we ?"

" Oh, I didn't mean that. Only it's generally the other way about, isn't it ? Men's barbers talk and ladies' hairdressers listen."

" He could write a book, the things women tell him. But I'm funny, dear, I'm not like that."

" Neither am I. But there is something in having your hair done. . . . Intimate, isolated and temporary. And looking in the mirror all the time. Seeing him only in the mirror. It's different."

" How cleverly you put it. I'm not a bit clever."

" When a woman doesn't talk about herself, well, I always think there's a reason, don't you ? Did you say your Russian was good looking ?"

" Not exactly, but arresting. And fine eyes."

" You must give me his address. I'm sick of my man."

" Of course, dear. But I can't promise anything. He doesn't generally do clients himself. He only advises."

" Well, I could try."

" I'm sure he'd make an exception of you if you told him you were a friend of mine."

" Thank you so much, dear. It's sweet of you."

" I sometimes think the only rest I get in the week is at the hairdresser's."

" You are looking a little tired, dear. But I thought you were rather dropping out. I didn't see you at the Thorleys' little do on Friday. I thought you always went there. You are great friends, aren't you ?"

" Len wouldn't go."

"And you gave in to him, dear, was that wise ?" Amy leaned forward a little, pushing aside her plate—the specialist in consultation.

" We had an awful row."

" You mustn't let him ride roughshod over you. Now is the time to make a stand. I don't have any trouble with Rex because he knows he can't do without me. He literally can't take a step in his business without my advice. I wouldn't tell everyone that. What I say is, don't trust to love. What you want is a hold over them."

" You're so clever."

" You don't think I'm butting in, do you, dear ?"

" Of course not, darling."

" I was so sorry you missed the party. It was very bright. I don't think George was in his usual form."

" Oh, wasn't he ?"

" They say she leads him a terrible life—but perhaps it's only malicious gossip. People will say anything."

" I happen to know it's true."

" What a pity. And he so popular — especially with women."

" He can't help his charm, can he ?. At heart he is very reserved."

" Oh, really ?"

The waitress laid the little yellow bill, decorously folded, in the exact centre of the table.

" Well, I suppose we'd better. . . It has been delightful seeing you, dear."

" There is nothing I love better than a good old talk."

" No, Amy, it's mine. I asked you."

" Oh, but, dear, it's my turn. You paid last time."

" Did I ? I don't remember."

" Neither do I, but I think you did."

" Well, if you only *think*, it is mine."

Their jewelled fingers met on the slip of paper. They smiled winningly at one another.

" Oh, well. . . . . "

They fumbled among the expensive furniture of their handbags, touched their noses solicitously with swansdown puffs, drew on white gloves, staring past one another, absorbed.

" Ready ?"

" Let's go."

They sailed out. A waitress waylaid them.

" I thought you'd paid. How silly of me."

" I thought you had. How absurd."

" Let me."

"All right, dear. It's too hot to quarrel."

They walked slowly down the shallow, thickly carpeted stairs, side by side.

" You promised me the address of your hairdresser."

" Yes, don't let me forget."

They stood a moment in the doorway before stepping into the bright river of the street. Lois caught Amy's arm.

" I want to ask you something. . . . I wouldn't ask if it wasn't perfectly all right. . . . Really I wouldn't. It's only that—would you mind saying that we'd 'been to a matinee together this afternoon ?"

Her eyes were wild, young, entreating in the perfect mask of her face.

DIALOGUE AT THE BALLET

The little girl sat as far back in her stall as she could, then she leaned forward a little ; in this way she was able to make her skirt cover her knees. Her legs, in black cotton stockings that had washed woolly, were tucked away under the seat, out of sight. Her hands, in the new cotton gloves Gran had bought her, were hidden under her hat which she held on her lap, the elastic wound round and round her forefinger till it had a funny, cold rubbery feeling, a no-feeling, blind and dumb. Her palms were pressed on the tight ball of her handkerchief, braced against it. She was, precariously safe like this, in a cave between the two large, opulent women who, smelling of powder and scent, of kid gloves and hair-dressers, bulged over her on either side in well-dressed curves. Her mind could dart out, like an ant-eater's tongue, and scoop in the amazing, lovely things that were happening on the bright stage in the great dark, hollow theatre. She was safe and even obscurely happy so long as they talked about Their Own Things and took no notice of her, Aunt Catherine and her friend Mrs. Furnival. Aunt Catherine wasn't a real Aunt, she was a godmother. Godmothers were like Santa Claus, you didn't believe in them, only pretended to, to please Mummie and Daddy. You couldn't call them Mrs. Orwell-Vane, you had apparently to say " aunt." Until today Aunt Catherine hadn't meant anything except a dented silver mug and the funny metallic taste of hot milk when you buried your nose in it to drink. It was Solid Silver. Mummie talked about someone called Kitty, who used to be Aunt Catherine but wasn't now. . .

When the lights went up, the little girl was taken by surprise just as she had been when they went out, but she didn't show it. She pressed hard on the handkerchief, and her eyes, which had been knobs in the darkness, suddenly flattened out. Aunt Catherine leaned towards her in a puff of warm air.

" We're enjoying ourselves enormously, aren't we ? Oh, I do wish I was a little girl seeing the ballet for the first time. I'd love to be a little girl again, wouldn't you, Melisande ?"

Mrs. Furnival had a name like barley sugar but she looked like a marshmallow.

" Did you see her eyes ? As big as saucers. I got more pleasure looking at her than at the stage."

" *Please Aunt Catherine, let me look for myself !*"

"The next Ballet is going to be the one you'll like. Look on the programme, dear. There. Cendrillon. That means Cinderella. Won't that be lovely ? You know the story, don't you. Of course, you do. Mumsie must have told it to you lots of times—and now you're going to see it. My, isn't that grand ?"

" Isn't she a quiet little country mouse ? Struck dumb
with wonder, I shouldn't be surprised. You know what
country children are like. Inarticulate, poor little thing.
What would you expect, living at the back of beyond ?
But we're marvellous friends already, aren't we, Bunny ?
I invented a pet name for her coming in in the taxi.
Yes, we had a taxi all the way from her grandmother's.
Talk about the wilds of suburbia ! Bunny. Her birth-
day's at Easter. Isn't it quaint ?"

" *You don't know rabbits like I do.*"

" Of course Nellie is a very nice name, but I wanted
something just special between ourselves."

" *She thinks Nellie is common.*"

" I went to school with her mother. The sweetest
thing. Plenty of money in those days but they lost it.
Why she wanted to bury herself right out there in the
bush I don't know. Love's young dream and all that,
poor darling. He never did much good. And then she
wanted me to be godmother to her first. So touching."

*Darling Mummie. Poor darling little mummie. I know
why. She wanted Aunt Catherine to do things for me.
And now she has. She's taking me to the ballet.*

" Four children and that climate. I ask you is any man
worth it ?"

*She thinks I'm deaf because I live in the bush. She'd
look awful on a horse. Daddy would laugh at her. We all
would.*

" The childie has come down to have her tonsils out.
Her first trip to town. I tell her it's going to be fun in
hospital after just the first tiny wee while, and she's as
brave as brave. She's ten years old. You'd hardly think
it, would you ?"

*Gran's giving me my operation. Day after to-morrow.
It won't be as bad as when the horse kicked me.*

" So I thought, even if it was a bit awkward for me
just now, I must give her a treat. Do you like your treat,
darling?"

" There, I've let the ice cream boy go by. Never mind.
We are going to have afternoon tea after the show.
Great big scrumptous cakes. How will you like that?"

*No one makes cakes like my mummy's. She won two prizes
in the show.*

" Funny little morsel, isn't it? Not a word to be got
out of her. I know she's having fun though. I know.
We understand one another."

" It's so good for her to see a little beauty. I believe
in filling their little minds with beautiful things, don't
you? It helps."

*There's Fancy licking her colt, and the willows by the
creek, and the new harvester, and the paddocks after rain.
I want to go home. It's awful here.*

" Would you like to go to the lav., pet? Sure? Quite
sure? It's no good being obstinate. All right, but it's
rude to shake your head like that. Say 'No thank you,
Aunt Catherine.' Here's the orchestra coming back. If
I were at my first ballet I'd be wild with excitement."

*Please don't smear talk all over it. Please let me see it
all by myself.*

" Look at the Sisters. Aren't they funny. . . . Well
I never, there's puss. . . . Isn't it dinky?. . . . Now
we're going to see the Fairy Godmother. . . . You've
got a fairy godmother too, haven't you?. . . . Don't
kick the seat, Nellie, it's rude. . . . Look, oh look. . . .
It's just the loveliest ballet, isn't it? . . . There's the

Prince. He's a girl really—or isn't he ? It's quite hard
to tell with some of these people. . . . Never mind. . . .
It's very pretty. . . . I could die laughing at those
Sisters. Clap, Bunny, clap hard to show you like it. Oh
dear, I'm afraid it's nearly over. I'm exhausted, Melisande, entertaining a child is hard work if you ask me.
God Save the King. Stand still and straight, pet. Don't
fidgit, it isn't loyal. There. Did you enjoy yourself ?
Did you ? She'll find her voice in a minute. Don't you
feel just a teeny, weeny bit like Cinderella yourself,
going to the ballet in a taxi with your godmother ? Eh,
chickie ?''

" No, I don't. I hated it,'' said the little girl in a sudden
loud voice, her face scarlet, her throat beginning to
swell with sobs.

THE PARTY

The footpath rang under her feet as if the hill were hollow. She had not been there before, and was convinced that she would not find her way. She stared incredulously at the street numbers and sought out, with a kind of fumbling desperation, like one learning braille, the landmarks that Rhonda had given her. She was late, and would probably be the last to arrive even at that sort of party. She had dawdled and dawdled, still thinging that perhaps she might not go, only in the end not going had proved worse than going. Not going would be a chasm of disappointment. It was enough to be late, she thought now, like the frightened man who believes his yawns will convince the world of his indifference.

This was the block of flats. An imitation stone staircase, mock baronial, mock grandeur, and behind the closed doors with their heavy antique knockers the same ordinary little flats, the same inescapable amenities. To the third floor. It wasn't only the stairs that made her heart beat so fast and high. It is shattering to go up to a smug, unknown door and ring the bell, knowing that a party lurks behind it. A close knit, if temporary, whole, a world whipped up out of conversation and sherry, to which she, the late comer, would be a stranger and an outcast, no matter how well she might know people. In the tight fitting, black frock that revealed so delicately the slender lines of her body, she felt that her heart was indecently exposed.

Well, she'd taken the plunge. A room full of people, all standing up, all holding wine glasses, talking as if they knew on another much better than they did, eating sausage rolls and gherkins. She knew at once. *John wasn't there.* There wasn't a hopeful corner of the room you couldn't see at the first glance.

Rhonda was beside her, in her eyes the look that said " My poor darling, how are you ?" The terrible, tender solicitude of a friend who knows and understands everything. But she only said, " I'll find Agnes for you." Old fashioned to be embarrassed because you did not know your hostess. But if I am I am, so what can I do about it? This was Agnes, wearing a snood. What incredible affectation to wear a snood at your own party as if you had just arrived out of the blue, and hadn't been cutting sandwiches and impaling little what-nots on toothpicks all the afternoon. " So very kind. . . " she said, and yes, she knew nearly everyone. Agnes you could see was the soul of kindness. Now she had gone to fetch someone. " You must meet. . . . so much in common." It was just as if she had said kindly, confidentially, " Now I'll go and get you a nice strong cup of tea and you will be all right." What she was likely to have in common with anyone, she couldn't imagine. She felt rather as she might have done if she had wandered into the party, wearing a diving bell. . . .

There was a solid wall of conversation, unscalable, impenetrable. " Mallarmé," someone said. So they still talked about Mallarmé at parties. " In Spain. . ." someone said. You always counted four points if you had been in Spain. Russia counted double, and London in the blitz came somewhere in between. You could be nostalgic over Paris, but not over London, for after all, London had taken it and Paris hadn't.

" My dear," said a strange young man solicitously. " You have nothing to drink."

With a wine glass in her hand, she felt herself immeasurably better equipped. Someone touched her arm.

She thought for a blind second that it might be John, but it was Agnes with the soul mate. A dark young man with a scar. She looked at him with an enquiring smile, and took a slow sip. That was better. She was getting the hang of it now. She would be able, after all, to give a very good imitation of herself this afternoon.

" You sculpt, don't you ?" he said.

" No," and then idiotically because it was like the snapping of a very thin life line. " I'm sorry. I would like to."

" You mean," he asserted, " that you do but you think you're only at the beginning. There isn't any beginning, only a circle."

" No," she said, fighting desperately now against the clay. " I mean no. I never thought of it. . . ."

" You have a sculptor's hands," he asserted.

In a moment it had become a nightmare conversation. She felt herself entangled in a net of meaningless words. She drifted into a group for protection, and when she drifted out she left him behind her.

" Darling, where have you been hiding ? I haven't seen you for ages."

" My dear, you are actually thinner, some people have all the luck."

" Don't slip away before I've told you what I'm doing. I've given up the violin and I'm working in a factory. It's more satisfactory. The pattern is so much thicker . . ."

No one even mentioned John. He might have been dead or forgotten, like a stone at the bottom of a well.

There was a picture on the wall, a red mouth with a Mona Lisa smile, set crookedly on a grey background. Just that and nothing more. A shutter flipped up in her mind and she saw it, really saw it. It was improbable but quite real. The solicitous young man stood before her, a plate in each hand. " Oyster patties or sausage rolls ?" It was one of those cryptic, irretrievable choices —heaven or hell and nothing to guide you. The casket scene. She wouldn't have either and he was disappointed to the point of despair. He had a beautiful maternal lust to feed people.

She moved on. She hadn't noticed the door behind the curtain. It came to softly behind her, leaving her in sudden quiet and enlargement. It was as easy to escape as that. The balcony, hanging like a bird cage on the clifflike facade of the flats, was as far from the party as Cape York. It was early dusk with its false evanescent clarity beginning to melt at the edges, a light that blent the noonday incompatibles into a scena. In the fore-ground, blocks of flats set at all angles, each flat a little box too small for the life it housed, so that it bulged out of the windows, hung over the balconies, burgeoned up through the roofs. Strings of coloured washing were as natural as vines. In William Street, narrow and living as an artery, coloured taxis moved like corpuscles. Over to the left, Woolloomooloo, pouring down the hill, houses, terraces, narrow streets fused into a solid mass, a grape bloom on its slates, a veil of light on the medioc-rity of its stones and bricks. Beneath the swept stretch of the waterfront, the wharves running neatly out into the bay. Beyond the lovely, unreal drop scene of the harbour, blue water, timbered headlands, even the bridge etherealised, a grey bow drawn across the blue.

Her constricted heart dilated as if to the sweep of music. She could stand and look for a minute, her palms pressed to the roughness of brick, forgetting everything. Then her mind began to tear at its knot again. " Why had John not come ? Was it because he thought she might be there ? Or for no reason so definite, because he had forgotten the occasion, the time or the place. . . . the indifference of his freedom in which everything eventually was lost !''

The dark young man with the scar had found the door too.

'' I lost you,'' he said.

That didn't need an answer, but she picked up her wine glass from the parapet.

'' Tell me,'' he said, '' what do you do ?''

'' Nothing,'' she said. '' That's killed it,'' she thought, and then, because that sudden sweep of music had left her defenceless, she began to tell him what she saw. '' If I lived here I'd throw a line out of the window every night, and every morning I'd haul in a short story.''

'' Writing.'' He drove the metal of his contempt into the word. '' That's no good. You can imagine anything at all and write it down. No limits and no discipline, it's only a hide-out for people who haven't anything to say.''

That didn't fetch her because he couldn't possibly say anything that touched her now. She felt indifference like a dead weight.

'' You're the sort,'' he said with the insolence of a man who succeeds with women, '' You're the sort who promises everything and gives nothing.''

In a small cold voice she said, '' I would like another glass of wine and something to eat.''

'' Certainly.'' He held the door for her to enter.

In the crowded room conversation was already in a more advanced state. One cannot afford to drop out. Talking is, like drinking, progressive. When you are a few drinks behind everyone else, you are in a different world.

Rhonda caught her fingers in a quick, affectionate squeeze. "It's a nice party, isn't it?" she said encouragingly.

It was a nice party.

"I'm so glad you clicked with Simon. He is doing something and going somewhere even if he is the world's greatest egoist."

The something in common.

She told Agnes that she had a dinner engagement, that she'd have to tear herself away.

One of the boys, Agnes said, would see her down. . . .

Please, please. . . . everyone was so happy. Let her just slip away. It was so easy to break up a party. . . .

She went into the bedroom. A stout woman had taken her shoes off because they hurt her, and was sitting on a low chair, smoking. Another was re-making her face very earnestly in a small mirror. Two more lounged on the bed. There was the intimate ease of women off parade, a freshet of laughter, a fragment of story like a tit-bit among gulls. Politely they suspended their conversation, politely made way for her. In the mirror she saw with surprise that the delicate mask of her make-up was still intact. She said good-bye, not remembering ever to have seen these women before.

She pulled the front door to after her. The air was suddenly cool, thin and flavoured with plaster. Three flights of imitation stone stairs, mock baronial, mock grandeur. In the street it was almost dark. She looked up and saw the lighted windows of the flat, golden in the blue dusk. She had left a world that, if it wasn't safe, was at least warm. It was being alone that was so terrible.

FIGHTING IN VIENNA

It was to buy bird-seed that Kathie, Fraulein von Hillse, decided to risk a journey through the streets. There was nothing left in the blue lacquered tin with the Japanese pagoda design that was almost worn off with long use. Long ago, before the war, when they were just beginning to be sweethearts, Johann had given her this tin filled with the most elegant little biscuits, nut shaped ones filled with chocolate paste, heart shapes covered with pink sugar crystals, candied violets in little baskets of macaroon. You didn't see things like that in Vienna now, not even for the rich tourists. It had just been one of many little gifts, hyacinths growing in pots, boxes of crystallised fruits, books, not very much heeded, but it had outlived them all. Even now Kathie could not handle it without a curious feeling as if a door somewhere had swung open, and the breath of a long dead springtime wafted across her senses. It stirred in her quite automatically a little pulse of homesickness, of nostalgia. Rather a faded emotion, but there.

Elsa coming at dusk yesterday with a basket of provisions, had not thought of canary seed. It was like Elsa to have come herself, to make nothing at all of the risk she ran. All through the dark years since the war Elsa had been the one fixed and steady light in Kathie's world—Elsa who could make sacrifices without repining, take burdens without comment, Elsa who had come yesterday through the dangerous streets with their sporadic fighting, which no one seemed able to foretell, to provision Kathie, so that she would not have to go out, even though she herself was distracted by fear and anxiety.

" Franz," she said slowly, her long white capable hands deftly unpacking the basket, " hasn't been home for two days." Then after a puase " Hermann is in Berlin. I've been to the hospitals. I'll try them again."

" Let me come with you," Kathie urged.

" It's easier for one. I'm less frightened alone," Elsa said. " I'll be quite safe, I know that." There was a note of despair in her voice as if she had tried to make a bargain with God, offering her life for her son's, and it had been refused.

Kathie had promised that she would stay quietly at home until things settled down, but now she was faced by the empty tin. It made her feel more forlorn, lonely, and shut up, than anything else had done. At last she really felt threatened. She looked at the bird in the cage, her little friend. It was natural for her to suffer, or so it seemed now, but not for him. She really did feel that he was her friend, her darling. When she came back to her small apartment each afternoon from the University, where Hermann, Elsa's husband, had got her a clerical job, he jumped about in his cage and chirped. He welcomed her. When she opened the cage as she often did, he fluttered round the room and came to perch on her hand. She loved the feel of his tiny fragile claws. He was not in the least afraid of her. She could even hold him in her closed hand and feel him vibrating with life and the tiny heart beating against her fingertips. He would draw his head back then and look at her first out of one beady eye and then out of the other, so knowing, so sure. And he sang. When Frau Müller worked the sewing machine in the room next door, when the sun came streaming into the room in the afternoon, and sometimes for no reason at all except that he was happy, song came pouring from his little throat. Yesterday, when the machine gun had been whining and stuttering in the street, he had tried to sing it down. Never had he sung so bravely. She almost feared his heart would burst.

Fraulein Kathie had a very strange thought about her bird sometimes, which she never told to anyone. It was that he was in some curious way herself, the gay and fortunate Kathie, who had been young and sought after and had loved Johann, long ago before the war. Nearly twenty years ago. It was as if the bird were her own singing heart so long silent in her breast. He was the happiness that was no longer hers, but yet shared her room with her. When he sang, something was released in her. Something that she thought would never answer again, replied to him.

Fraulein Kathie put on her hat and coat. After all it was not far to Schlesmann's shop where she could buy the seed and a chillie or two. She opened the shutter a little and looked out. The street was very quiet—shuttered windows, bolted doors, tight lipped house with blank faces, no one passing to and fro. There hadn't been any firing since yesterday. That hadn't been so very terrible either, just some rifle shots and then the nervous rattle and stutter of the machine gun. There had been nothing to see even then but dust in the street, some fallen plaster from a cornice, and a dark, insignificant looking huddle of clothes at the corner that was nevertheless a man's body. Kathie had not been frightened or excited—only, when the bird sang, a little exalted. Emotions did not come readily to her now. It was as if she had to lift a weight off her heart before she could feel anything. All her emotions, even the pride and joy she felt in the brilliant boy, Franz, even her fear for him now, came to her slowly and with difficulty.

It was strange in the deserted streets. Kathie remembered a day when she was a child and instead of going to school, had run away to play alone under the lilacs in the Stadtpark, to walk alone, guilty and happy, through the white surf of daisies on the spring lawns. Even the air had felt different on her cheek. It did today.

It was only a few minutes walk to Schlesmann's shop. When she got there the door was shut and planks had been roughly nailed over the one small window. The broken glass was swept up against the wall. Peering between the boards Kathie saw the trampled litter of the interior. It had been looted. Poor old Schlesmann, what had become of him ? Kathie went on, a few blocks away there was another little shop.

Here was a house that she knew well. It had been burnt, and on all the neighbouring walls were pale furrows and nicks where bullets had passed. Round the next corner she found a barricade across the street and a posse of soldiers. Kathie stopped, not quite knowing what to do. A young lieutenant came towards her. " You cannot pass this way, Fraulein. If you are wise you will go home." He spoke to her quietly and courteously. He was a nice boy, she thought, not more than twenty years old, a true Viennese, fair oval face, full lips and heavy lidded eyes. Kathie moved away obediently in the direction she had come.

Then a sudden thought came and she stood still, shocked. The young lieutenant reminded her of Franz. And they, Franz and he, were enemies. Franz was a rebel, he who had never suffered anything in his own person, who was protected by his father's position but must generously, recklessly throw himself into a lost cause, flinging himself against the iron wall of the new

tyrany to make a new world where, her sick heart told
her, not even the materials of a new world were left.
Franz, making them all unhappy, despising his father's
money for the way it was earned, although he couldn't
escape its benefit, despising his mother for her marriage,
although it had meant his birth, not understanding at
all the sacrifice she had made, that she continued to make.
Franz and that young lieutenant cancelling out.

Kathie walked on quickly. Presently she came out in
the Ring, the wide boulevarde that circles the heart of
Vienna and runs where the old city wall used to stand.
Here there was more traffic but not much, swift closed
cars, a lorry with soldiers, a few pedestrians. The handsome buildings, that lined it, looked serenely down. "The
lovely shell of Vienna," thought Kathie, " but there is
no health or prosperity left in her." That seemed an old,
old thought.

She would cross the Ring in the direction of the Prater ;
there were plenty of small shops there in the labyrinth
of streets. They could not all have been looted. She
would tap on a side door, buy her seed furtively and
quickly and hurry home. Already she was feeling tired.
There was tension in these unnaturally quiet streets.

A young man began to run. In the distance, from the
direction of the University, Kathie heard several shots.
A church bell, wild, terrible, insistant, began to ring,
clashing and clamouring. Under its lightning there came
presently the thunder of lorries. There was now a nervous staccato fusilade of shots. Presently the machine
guns would start. That was how it began, this feverish,
sporadic fighting. First a dead calm, silent, waiting, an
isolated shot or two, then almost at once a frenzy of
excitement, a sort of nerve storm, hysterical courage and
wanton destruction. No one seemed to know from which

house the firing might begin at any time. The conflict had no definite outlines, it came and went like an ague, more a matter of nerves than passion. When it died down again, the ambulances came and took the wounded to the hospitals, the dead to the morgue, the fire brigade turned out and extinguished the fires. The police nailed planks over shattered windows, and cleared the glass out of the way. They even went about arresting people. All neat and orderly and according to regulations.

Kathie stood on the kerb nervously buttoning and un-buttoning her glove. In a moment everything was changed, people were running, mounted troops, coming at the gallop, followed lorries with machine guns, other bells further away, began to ring. Behind the troops came two ambulances. Kathie began to walk with nervous, jerky steps in the direction of the University. She had no very clear idea of what she was doing, the wild clamour of the bells in her ears dazed her. All at once they stopped and the sound of the fighting crackled and blazed on the tingling silence. Nobody noticed Fraulein Kathie. There were a lot of soldiers about, but no one told her to go back. She had a confused idea that she ought to do some-thing, that now at last she was going to wake from her dumb, hurt lethargy. She would do her part. Perhaps Franz was down there, she would find him and bring him home ; perhaps he was hurt.

It all happened around the University, familiar ground, where she had gone to work each day until the Univer-sity was closed by the Authorities a fortnight ago. She was nearer now and could see what was happening. The students had made a sortie and were fighting fiercely round one of the army lorries for a machine gun. They were evidently in possession of one of the buildings, and firing from the windows. The machine gun was silent.

Kathie could hear the words of command quite clearly, saw the soldiers kneeling to fire into the crowd. " Why," she thought, " I'm in action !"

So this was what it was like. She thought of Johann, who was dead, and Franz, who was lost, and of the bird in the cage at home, singing his little heart out. She did not feel afraid. A bullet hit the wall behind her, then another one, glancing off again. She felt a sudden fiery stab between her shoulders and for a second did not understand what had happened. Someone was running towards her. She thought it was Franz or the young lieutenant. Then blackness bubbled up in her throat and she fell.

. . . .

The sun crept across the face of the apartment building and, finding the chink in the shutter, streamed into Fraulein Kathie's deserted room. It fell on the table, where the empty tin with the pagoda design lay, it touched the faded photo of a young man in uniform, found the bird cage on the wall. The room had been dim and silent all day, the canary had hopped about on the floor of his cage picking up the seeds he usually despised. Now he sang.

Frau Müller, in the room across the passage, said " There's that bird." She went over and tapped at Fraulein von Hillse's door. It was still locked. " She'll have gone to her sister's," she thought. "It's well to have rich relations these days, though I don't know that I'd like a Nazi for a brother-in-law."

The sun passed on. The bird did not sing again that day.

. . . .

Kathie lay in the hospital. She did not know anything as definite as that. She was wrapped in a thick hot haze

She was made of haze herself, and would float away except that a red hot stake was driven through her. She tried to get free because there was something she must do. It was terribly important, but she did not know what it was. The more she struggled the more it hurt. Red flames mounting in the night, flames like bells.

" I must sing," thought Kathie.

The doctor asked the sister if the patient had recovered consciousness.

" No, Herr Doktor."

" And you do not know who she is yet ?"

" No, Herr Doktor, there have been no enquiries yet."

The doctor held the lanquid hand, taking the pulse. He made a little significant grimace and exchanged a glance with the sister. There was something final in the way he laid Kathie's hand down again on the bed.

The sister was emboldened to ask him a question, although it was against the etiquette of the occasion.

" Herr Doktor, how is the boy in No. 27 ?"

The doctor answered negligently but without offence, " He'll recover all right but he may lose his hand. The bomb, you know. . . ."

They moved on to the next bed.

. . . .

There was only a drop of water left in the small vessel hooked on to the side of the canary's cage, and there was no seed left at all. Yet when, on the third afternoon of his loneliness the sunbeam through the chink in the shutter reached him, he sang again, lifting his head and ruffling his feathers. Frau Müller did not hear him, for she had fled from Vienna. Nobody was to hear him sing again.

. . . .

In the confusion of pain and darkness that was Kathie's mind a little space cleared, a rift of shining clarity. It seemed to be not in herself but in the sky above her, something she must struggle towards. Her eyes were open, she turned her head very slowly from side to side. The sister came to her bed and bent over her, a clear young face between the folds of her coif. Kathie struggled with a question. She wanted to ask if Franz had been found. The words seemed to waver like smoke from her lips, but she heard herself say, " Johann. . . . where is he ? Is he all right ?"

" He's all right," said the sister soothingly.

Kathie remembered. She had seen him running towards her in the street but he had been in uniform. Something terrible had been happening. Her struggling, questioning eyes remained fixed on the sister's face. The girl bent closer and said clearly and slowly, " Johann is safe and well. It's all right."

Kathie felt cool light spread over her. She understood. She had been ill. This was a hospital. She had been very ill for a long time and had terrible dreams. She had thought Johann was dead. She knew just where the bad dream had begun. She was with Elsa in their little sitting room. Elsa's long golden plaits fell one over each shoulder. Mama said, " Elsa, when will you put your hair up ? You are too old to wear it like that."

" But I don't want to grow up, Mama," cried Elsa. " I want to stay just like this for ever and ever." And she began to twirl round the room humming a waltz.

There was a ring at the front door, a long, loud, masculine ring. " There's Johann come to take you riding in the Prater," said Elsa. But it was not Johann, it was Hermann to see Elsa. Elsa turned away, flushing and naughty. " I won't see him," she said. " Tell him I've gone into a convent, and have smallpox."

While they had been laughing and whispering Johann had come in. He looked so changed, older and sterner. He had terrible news. The Archduke Franz Ferdinand had been assassinated at Serajevo. The air seemed to clot about them. " This will mean war," said Johann. She fingered the braid on his breast and put her arms round his neck, to hold him. What agony to lift her arms, a pain that dashed in a surf upon her brain, blotting out all thought.

Kathie's lips were moving, but no one could hear what she said. She was talking to Johann, and the words seemed to run straight out of her heart without the effort of speaking.

" Darling, darling, darling, I've had such a bad dream. Your hand, Liebchen, I thought you'd lost your right hand. You came back from the war and there was nothing for you, only me, and I wasn't enough." Kathie tried to laugh, but she couldn't do that just yet. "Your father was dead and there wasn't any money and what could you do with only one hand, and so many men with two hands looking for work ? Little Elsa married Hermann—I thought that too—she did it to save us all from going under, starving perhaps, and we let her although we hated the way Hermann got his money, out of everyone's suffering. Such a terrible, dark, defeated winter, darling. The worst thing of all was that I couldn't help you, Johann. I wanted you to marry me and let Elsa help us to live somehow, just cower together in a tiny, tiny room, keeping one another alive, keeping our little flame of love and happiness alive till times got better. You wouldn't, Johann. I thought if I loved you enough I could make up for everything. But I couldn't. You'd been through too much to want love. You couldn't love or hope. But you were so quiet and gentle.

Just sat with your useless arm . . . Life couldn't ever have
been as bad as that dream, could it, Johann ? Things
like that couldn't happen really, could they ? God
wouldn't let them. You didn't even tell me what was in
your mind, you tried to comfort me. Then it was spring
again. The lilac came out just as usual as if nothing had
happened that winter. I could smell it in the streets
and I thought, walking home, that everything would be
better now. I'd get you out into the sunshine and you'd
be healed. But you weren't at home, you weren't anywhere, you'd thrown yourself into the canal, like so
many others. . . ."

A low, moaning cry came from Kathie's lips. " Poor
soul," thought the old woman in the next bed, " if only
she could go."

. . . .

That day the canary did not sing. He sat huddled on
the perch, his beak open, gasping. A fine dust had settled
on everything in the room, even, it seemed, on the eyes
of the bird.

. . . .

Miraculously, Elsa was there beside the bed, holding
her hand, calling her name, forcing her up through turbid
waters. Five days had changed Kathie very much, her
face was shrunk and small, her lips cracked with fever.
Her eyes, dark and troubled, looked from another world.

There was a white screen around the bed, and, although
she smiled, Elsa was weeping. The sister stood beside her.

There was an immense question in Kathie's eyes. Her
spirit was saying to her body," Why are you suffering
so ? Can I be dying ?" But they did not know that.
Elsa tried to answer that look.

" Franz is safe," she said slowly, distinctly. " He's

here. He was hurt the day you were. His poor hand. . . .
but he won't die."

"Johann," whispered Kathie.

"I'll take him right away from Vienna. We'll begin
again." The sister made a little warning movement.

Kathie's mind was pulling itself free, with terrible
agonising jerks coming back to reality. She must tell
Elsa about the empty tin.

"I couldn't," she whispered. "Schlesmann's. . . ."

"What did she say," asked Elsa. The sister shook
her head.

Kathie was trying to raise herself, beating agonised
hands against the pain and the darkness. "He sang,"
she said quite clearly.

Then the stake was drawn out of her breast. She was
free. There rose in her a fountain of blood, of tears, of
song.

. . . .

A small untidy heap of ruffled feathers lay on the floor
of the bird cage, the tiny, claw-like feet stood stiffly up.
The sunlight found only silence and dust. Outside, the
street was awaking, shutters were opened cautiously,
vehicles passed. Life began again.

THE LOTTERY

The first that Ted Bilborough knew of his wife's good fortune was when one of his friends, an elderly wag, shook his hand with mock gravity and murmured a few words of manly but inappropriate sympathy. Ted didn't know what to make of it. He had just stepped from the stairway on to the upper deck of the 6.15 p.m. ferry from town. Fred Lewis seemed to have been waiting for him, and as he looked about he got the impression of newspapers and grins and a little flutter of half derisive excitement, all focused on himself. Everything seemed to bulge towards him. It must be some sort of leg pull. He felt his assurance threatened, and the corner of his mouth twitched uncomfortably in his fat cheek, as he tried to assume a hard boiled manner.

" Keep the change, laddie," he said.

" He doesn't know, actually he doesn't know."

" Your wife's won the lottery !"

" He won't believe you. Show him the paper. There it is as plain as my nose. Mrs. Grace Bilborough, 52 Cuthbert Street." A thick, stained forefinger pointed to the words. " First prize £5000 Last Hope Syndicate."

" He's taking it very hard," said Fred Lewis, shaking his head.

They began thumping him on the back. He had travelled on that ferry every week-day for the last ten years, barring a fortnight's holiday in January, and he knew nearly everyone. Even those he didn't know entered into the spirit of it. Ted filled his pipe nonchalantly but with unsteady fingers. He was keeping that odd unsteadyness, that seemed to begin somewhere deep in his chest, to himself. It was a wonder that fellows in the office hadn't got hold of this, but they had been busy today in the hot loft under the chromium pipes of the pneumatic system, sending down change and checking up on credit accounts. Sale time. Grace might have let him know. She could have rung up from Thompson's. Bill was always borrowing the lawn mower and the step ladder, so it would hardly be asking a favour in the circumstances. But that was Grace all over.

" If I can't have it myself, you're the man I like to see get it."

They meant it too. Everyone liked Ted in a kind sort of way. He was a good fellow in both senses of the word. Not namby pamby, always ready for a joke but a good citizen too, a good husband and father. He wasn't the sort that refused to wheel the perambulator. He flourished the perambulator. His wife could hold up her head, they payed their bills weekly and he even put something away, not much but something, and that was a triumph the way things were, the ten per cent knocked off his salary in the depression not restored yet, and one thing and another. And always cheerful, with a joke for everyone. All this was vaguely present in Ted's mind. He'd always expected in a trusting sort of way to be rewarded, but not through Grace.

" What are you going to do with it, Ted ?"

" You won't see him for a week, he's going on a jag." This was very funny because Ted never did, not even on Anzac Day.

A voice with a grievance said, not for the first time " I've had shares in a ticket every week since it started, and I've never won a cent." No one was interested.

" You'll be going off for a trip somewhere ?"

" They'll make you president of the Tennis Club and you'll have to donate a silver cup."

They were flattering him underneath the jokes.

" I expect Mrs. Bilborough will want to put some of it away for the children's future," he said. It was almost as if he were giving an interview to the press, and he was pleased with himself for saying the right thing. He always referred to Grace in public as Mrs. Bilborough. He had too nice a social sense to say " the Missus."

Ted let them talk, and looked out of the window. He wasn't interested in the news in the paper tonight. The little boat vibrated fussily, and left a long wake like moulded glass in the quiet river. The evening was drawing in. The sun was sinking into a bank of grey cloud, soft and formless as mist. The air was dusky, so that its light was closed into itself and it was easy to look at, a thick golden disc more like a moon rising through smoke than the sun. It threw a single column of orange light on the river, the ripples from the ferry fanned out into it, and their tiny shadows truncated it. The bank, rising steeply from the river and closing it in till it looked like a lake, was already bloomed with shadows. The shapes of two churches and a broken frieze of pine trees stood out against the gentle sky, not sharply, but with a soft arresting grace. The slopes, wooded and scattered with houses, were dim and sunk in idyllic peace. The river showed thinly bright against the dark land. Ted could see that the smooth water was really a pale tawny gold with patches, roughened by the turning tide, of frosty blue. It was only when you stared at it and concentrated your attention that you realised the colours. Turning to look down stream away from the sunset, the water gleamed silvery grey with dark clear scrabblings upon it. There were two worlds, one looking towards the sunset with the dark land against it dreaming and still, and the other looking down stream over the silvery river to the other bank, on which all the light concentrated. Houses with windows of orange fire, black trees, a great silver gasometer, white oil tanks with the look of clumsy mushrooms, buildings serrating the sky, even a suggestion seen or imagined of red roofs, showing up miraculously in that airy light.

" Five thousand pounds," he thought. " Five thousand pounds." Five thousand pounds at five per cent, five thousand pounds stewing gently in its interest, making old age safe. He could do almost anything he could think of with five thousand pounds. It gave his mind a stretched sort of feeling, just thinking of it. It was hard to connect five thousand pounds with Grace. She might have let him know. And where had the five and three-pence to buy the ticket come from ? He couldn't help wondering about that. When you budgeted as carefully as they did there wasn't five and threepence over. If there had been, well, it wouldn't have been over at all, he would have put it in the bank. He hadn't noticed any difference in the housekeeping, and he prided himself he noticed everything. Surely she hadn't been running up bills to buy lottery tickets. His mind darted here and there suspiciously. There was something secretive in Grace, and he'd thought she told him everything. He'd taken it for granted, only, of course, in the ordinary run there was nothing to tell. He consciously relaxed the knot in his mind. After all, Grace had won the five thousand pounds. He remembered charitably that she had always been a good wife to him. As he thought that he had a vision of the patch on his shirt, his newly washed cream trousers laid out for tennis, the children's neatness, the tidy house. That was being a good wife. And he had been a good husband, always brought his money home and never looked at another woman. Their's was a model home, everyone acknowledged it, but—well—somehow he found it easier to be cheerful in other people's homes than in his own. It was Grace's fault. She wasn't cheery and easy going. Something moody about her now. Woody. He'd worn better than Grace, anyone could see that, and yet it was he who had had the hard time. All she had to do was to stay at home and look after the house and the children. Nothing much in that. She always seemed to be working, but he couldn't see what there was to do that could take her so long. Just a touch of woman's perversity. It wasn't that Grace had aged. Ten years married and with two children, there was still something girlish about her—raw, hard girlishness that had never mellowed. Grace was—Grace, for better or for worse. Maybe she'd be a bit brighter now. He could not help wondering how she had managed the five and three. If she could shower five and threes about like that, he'd been giving her too much for the housekeeping. And why did she want to give it that damnfool name " Last Hope." That meant there had been others, didn't it ? It probably didn't mean a thing, just a lucky tag.

A girl on the seat opposite was sewing lace on silkies for her trousseau, working intently in the bad light. " Another one starting out," Ted thought.

" What about it ?" said the man beside him.

Ted hadn't been listening.

The ferry had tied up at his landing stage and Ted got off. He tried not to show in his walk that his wife had won £5000. He felt jaunty and tired at once. He walked up the hill with a bunch of other men, his neighbours. They were still teasing him about the money, they didn't know how to stop. It was a very still, warm evening. As the sun descended into the misty bank on the horizon it picked out the delicate shapes of clouds invisibly sunk in the mass, outlining them with a fine thread of gold.

One by one the men dropped out, turning into side streets or opening garden gates till Ted was alone with a single companion, a man who lived in a semi-detached cottage at the end of the street. They were suddenly very quiet and sober. Ted felt the ache round his mouth where he'd been smiling and smiling.

" I'm awfully glad you've had this bit of luck."

" I'm sure you are, Eric," Ted answered in a subdued voice.

" There's nobody I'd sooner see have it."

" That's very decent of you."

" I mean it."

" Well, well, I wasn't looking for it."

" We could do with a bit of luck like that in our house."

" I bet you could."

" There's an instalment on the house due next month, and Nellie's got to come home again. Bob can't get anything to do. Seems as if we'd hardly done paying for the wedding."

" That's bad."

" She's expecting, so I suppose Mum and Dad will be let in for all that too."

" It seems only the other day Nellie was a kid getting round on a scooter."

" They grow up," Eric agreed. " It's the instalment that's the rub. First of next month. They expect it on the nail too. If we hadn't that hanging over us it wouldn't matter about Nellie coming home. She's our girl, and it'll be nice to have her about the place again."

" You'll be as proud as a cow with two tails when you're a grandpa."

" I suppose so."

They stood mutely by Eric's gate. An idea began to flicker in Ted's mind, and with it came a feeling of sweetness and happiness and power such as he had never expected to feel.

" I won't see you stuck, old man," he said.

" That's awfully decent of you."

" I mean it."

They shook hands as they parted. Ted had only a few steps more and he took them slowly. Very warm and dry, he thought. The garden will need watering. Now he was at his gate. There was no one in sight. He stood for a moment looking about him. It was as if he saw the house he had lived in for ten years, for the first time. He saw that it had a mean, narrow-chested appearance. The roof tiles were discoloured, the woodwork needed painting, the crazy pavement that he had laid with such zeal had an unpleasant flirtatious look. The revolutionary thought formed in his mind. " We might leave here." Measured against the possibilities that lay before him, it looked small and mean. Even the name, " Emoh Ruo," seemed wrong, pokey.

Ted was reluctant to go in. It was so long since anything of the least importance had happened between him and Grace, that it made him shy. He did not know how she would take it. Would she be all in a dither and no dinner ready ? He hoped so but feared not.

He went into the hall, hung up his hat and shouted in a big bluff voice " Well, well, well, and where's my rich wife ?"

Grace was in the kitchen dishing dinner.

" You're late," she said. "The dinner's spoiling."

The children were quiet but restless, anxious to leave the table and go out to play. " I got rid of the reporters," Grace said in a flat voice. Grace had character, trust her to handle a couple of cub reporters. She didn't seem to want to talk about it to her husband either. He felt himself, his voice, his stature dwindling. He looked at her with hard eyes. " Where did she get the money," he wondered again, but more sharply.

Presently they were alone. There was a pause. Grace began to clear the table. Ted felt that he must do something. He took her awkwardly into his arms. " Gracie, aren't you pleased ?"

She stared at him a second then her face seemed to fall together, a sort of spasm, something worse than tears. But she twitched away from him. "Yes," she said, picking up a pile of crockery and making for the kitchen. He followed her.

" You're a dark horse, never telling me a word about it."

" She's like a Red Indian," he thought. She moved about the kitchen with quick nervous movements. After a moment she answered what was in his mind :

" I sold mother's ring and chain. A man came to the door buying old gold. I bought a ticket every week till the money was gone."

" Oh," he said. Grace had sold her mother's wedding ring to buy a lottery ticket.

" It was my money."

" I didn't say it wasn't."

" No, you didn't."

The plates chattered in her hands. She was evidently feeling something, and feeling it strongly. But Ted didn't know what. He couldn't make her out.

She came and stood in front of him, her back to the littered table, her whole body taut. " I suppose you're wondering what I'm going to do ? I'll tell you. I'm going away. By myself. Before it is too late. I'm going tomorrow."

He didn't seem to be taking it in.

" Beattie will come and look after you and the children. She'll be glad to. It won't cost you a penny more than it does now," she added.

He stood staring at her, his flacid hands hanging down, his face sagging.

" Then you meant what it said in the paper, " Last Hope ?" he said.

" Yes," she answered.

SUNDAY

John preferred to walk up from the ferry. The empty bus passed him on the hill, its thick purr gradually diminishing as if it were slowly soaking into the golden morning. He lifted his head to the silence. He was not used to it, it made him feel as if he were on a height, a slight, delicious giddiness between his eyes and the crown of his head. The sunlight seeped into him, but it was backed by a small cold breeze, the westerly that gave the day its clear brilliance, so that he was conscious of his body inside his clothes, oddly vulnerable, and of himself as a dark stroke on the flawless autumn day. It was his body and not his mind that felt selfconscious, and he remembered that it was always like that when he returned. He had woken up that morning loathing everything. He had been repelled by yesterday's staleness, yesterday's cigarette butts and stacked washing up, the longstanding frowsiness of a man living alone in poverty, with which he had been shut up all night. The half-written story too, which was giving him so much trouble, hung like a murk in the room. His mind had shut against it in a nervous despair with which he was all too familiar. His loathing had been like a bad taste in his mouth. He had been glad to step out of it and turn the key upon it. That was why he was earlier than usual, that and because he hated to be expected, to see his mother waiting for him at the gate in her apron.

Now he came on the house unawares. He stood and stared for a moment at the cottage before he went in, fingering again his conscious detachment like a coin in his pocket. There was the picket fence, the two pine trees that ate all the good out of the soil, and covered

the thin grass with brown needles, the wide gateless side
entrance, dusty and rutted with the passage of the vans,
the peeling board above it with the words "Removalist"
and "General Carrier" scarcely distinguishable, the
stables, his father's boxlike office of unpainted wood, the
bare paddock beyond where the horses were spelled ;
on the other side of the house, the private side, the garden,
heavy headed dahlias, chrysanthemums rank smelling,
the cassia bush a blob of bright yellow, a thich ball of
flowers, little paths edged with glazed tiles and beds
bordered with fleshy rosettes of "cups-and-saucers."
The cottage was wide, low, drab and of weatherboard,
the windows shut, the steps whitened almost startlingly
in the general drabness. It looked quiet, uninhabited.
John knew it was readied up, waiting as ever for something that never happened, waiting for a funeral perhaps,
for nothing less would be allowed to disturb it. That or
Connie's wedding. A funeral was inevitable some day,
Connie's wedding wasn't. All the life was at the back of
the house. He went round the house on the stable side
because he did not want to meet his father.

He went up the two steps into the big old-fashioned
kitchen. His mother was at the sink with the tap turned
on, washing the vegetables, and did not hear him, but
she felt his shadow darken the door. She turned.

"Why, Jackie, you startled me." She dried her hands
hastily on her apron as he kissed her. "And I wasn't
at the gate to meet you," she added self-reproachfully.
"You're early, love." Her voice was as flat as the felt
slippers she wore to ease her bunions, but her worn hands
trembled a little as she put them on her son's shoulders.

"How are you, Mum ?"

"I'm all right, son."

She didn't ask any questions, but she looked them, searching him with her eyes. She knew that she must make the most of this moment when she had him to herself. He rubbed his cheek against her's to escape her eyes. He knew that she forgave him because his cuffs were frayed and his tie worn to a string, but it irked him that she should forgive him when there was nothing to forgive. I forgive you, my son, for living your own life, because I see it is a failure and that you are suffering for it. I forgive you for being my mother and for loving me. I love you.

It was over. Connie came in. " Hullo, Jack." She had washed her hair and had been drying it in the sun, a bath towel round her shoulders. He kissed her. The sewing machine stopped in the box room off the kitchen, and Izzie came in. " Hullo, Jack. I thought I heard you." Izzie was tall with faded, untidy, red hair. She had come years ago when the children were small, a child herself, as " mother's help " and now was an indissoluble part of the family. John kissed her too.

" I'll make the tea," said the mother, lifting the lid of the range and setting the black iron kettle down on the bright fire. " Your father's on the side verandah."

He went out into the sun again with Connie, while Izzie set out the cups.

They walked in silence between the dahlias. Connie pressed back the damp hair from her high bumpy forehead. She didn't care how she looked, but why should she ? He was her brother. You would hardly think she was two years younger than he, a woman still in her twenties. It was this that aroused his affection. He wanted to make contact with her. Why shouldn't they be frank with one another ?

" How are things ?" he asked.

"Same as usual."

"School?"

"Oh, school—different every day and always the same."
A dark discontent settled on her face.

"Why don't you cut out of it?"

"What's the good? Anything else would be the same."

That sounded like a dead end, but he was really thinking about himself.

"You and I are alike, Connie, only I've got free and
you haven't."

"Have you?" she asked dryly, looking him up and
down.

"Is that how you measure everything?" he asked,
nettled.

She laughed, and tried to pull his arm through hers.
It was Connie's way to be disagreable first, and friendly
afterwards, when it was too late. The thought of defen-
ding his position exhausted him. He would never make
her understand that being a failure his own way was a
sort of freedom, that he might be making a poor showing
now, but that he was slowly gathering himself for something else, that what he needed was nothingness, a rest
from importunities. He had shaken off the importunities
of his home, the loving kindness of his mother, which he
could not resist, the dominence of his father, the perpetual insistance of his father's will that he, for some
complex reason, in which perhaps being the eldest child
had its part, could not resist at short range either. He
had taken on other importunities that humbled and
interrupted him, but did not penetrate his spirit in the
same way. Creation could still come to him. He was
free, at least, in whatever poverty and distress, to give
his mind to that long brooding, when it hung like a drop
over a precipice ready to fall. How could he say that to

any human being, least of all to Connie ? She didn't
know that there was a difference between success in the
carrying trade, and success in writing. He might just as
well offer his father a mystic experience as a reason for
not going into the family business. He wasn't, he told
himself glancing at his sister, waterproof like Connie.
She could go into herself and shut the door. She didn't
need a desert and a cell. She would never do anything
so jejune as to rebel—jejune was the word she would use
—because her conception of the trap was so much more
complete than his. No futile childish rebellion could
liberate her. They gave up the discussion now with
nothing said. All family conversation, it seemed, was of
this stunted growth.

" Hadn't you better go and see father ?" she asked
with a trace of malice.

John went round to the side verandah, where his father
sat on a deck chair in the sun, behind the knotted, leafless
screen of the wistaria, the Sunday paper strewed about
him, a large dominant old man with jutting brows and a
thick mouth. It was a shock to John each time he saw
his father, to realise that he was an old man, but the
impression, when they talked, always wore off again.
They met quite casually now. The old man was aware
that this was only a truce, this visit, a concession to
family feeling. He was ready to concede something to
family feeling even in the most strained circumstances.
Perhaps he concealed from himself that he no longer had
the impetus to quarrel with his son.

Presently the mother came out with the tea in breakfast
cups on a large papier mache tray. There were plates of
buttered scones and rock cakes. " Don't spoil your
dinner," she said tenderly, pressing John to eat.

The old man went on reading his paper and she went away but soon appeared again, the father's dressing gown over her arm, and beckoned conspiratorially to John. "Let me press your suit." Obediently he took the dressing gown, and went into the room that used to be his.

He stood beside the bed that had been made up. Perhaps his mother had though he would stay, or it might have been made for someone else. He longed to lay his head upon the pillow. It was clean without spot or blemish. He turned down a corner of the coverlet and, thrust his hand, which looked very dark against their whiteness, between the coarse, clean linen sheets. He was swept by an agony of longing for peace and security such as he had never known since he was born. The burden of his manhood was intolerable. The linen, its homeliness, its cleanness, made him aware of his mother, of his loneliness, that he was forever a stranger to that ragged edge of world where he lived, and to the rootless and necessitious gaiety which was not gaiety, but a fumbling after stimulation. He revolted against his portion, contacts without background, the always shifting pattern, long stimulation without climax, a world drained to its patter. He stared at his dark hand, in the trance to which a mind long forced, gives way. He let a pain for which he had no name flow through him unimpeded, in the widening hope, the belief of a child who has always been protected, that it would work out its own solution, that so much feeling must be shaped to something.

He pulled off his coat, vest, trousers. If he did not go out his mother would come in to look for him, and that would be intolerable. The kitchen greeted him with a sunny blast, and the warm aroma of dinner now far advanced. His mother had the ironing board set up across the window, the iron heated. " Wouldn't you like to go inside and sit down ?" she asked as if he were a visitor. No, he liked the kitchen much better. He sat down on the wooden kitchen chair.

The moment of crisis was over, gone like a wave. Vaguely he missed it, felt himself comfortably rocked in the weakness of strain relaxed, about him the indulgence of a convalescent. He looked out of the open door at the shadow of a creeper on the worn bricks. That was good. The delicate twining pattern satisfied him, the creeper itself was indeterminate, the shadow completed and perfect. He could not lift his mind away from it. His mother ejaculated scraps of family news between thumps of the iron. " Betty's expecting again," she said. Betty was his brother's wife. He'd married her four months before their first child was born, but everyone had for-gotten that now—except perhaps Vic. Already at twenty-four he looked like a man who had worked hard, with a puzzled, patient look about his forehead. That thought bobbed past John's mind like a cork on water, and went away. " She'll be able to use nearly all Bubby's things, she kept them so nice."

Izzie moved from dresser to table, from table to oven. She made a noise whatever she touched. She interjected her comments into the conversation. Connie passed in and out, calling out remarks over her shoulder. Steam rose up from the wet cloth, as the mother pressed the suit. Every now and then she put the iron aside and went to the range, shouldering Izzie away as if she were jealous in the preparation of the dinner. John has seen this muted, domestic hostility between them before. It seemed part of the natural rightness of everything here. He knew that he loved above all things the comfortable shabbiness of his home. It wasn't the shabbiness of shoddy things gone while they were still new, but of old friends who had worn a long time. Everything in the kitchen, he saw now, was too big for the family—the big boilers on the stove, the black iron kettles, the copper saucepans. Even the dinner plates with their ugly brown pattern and criss-cross of tiny cracks were an out size. He had never known any others. They comforted him. He didn't listen to what anyone said.

There were steps on the path outside. " That'll be Gwennie," said his mother. He might have known she'd have Gwen here.

Gwen came in with an armful of tight yellow chrysan-themums. She looked just the same as when she left school ten years ago. She had a little snub nose, gentle and confiding, with a scatter of freckles across it, and tight curled hair that looked as if it would crackle under the hand. She wore a blue serge dress with a velvet collar.

" Hullo, Gwen," he said, and got up and kissed her. It was as if he had kissed the chrysanthemums, for he got no impression but of their pungency.

" Oh, Jack," she said in her little breathless voice.

" I brought you some chrysanths," she said kissing his mother.

He saw how well they understood one another. It was obvious to him that Gwen, backed up by his mother, was waiting for him, till in some mysterious way, he " came round." He suspected that the old lady even hoped he might get into a scrape with her like Vic had, and have to marry her. Better that way than not at all. It would be all for the best. He'd be roped down then, settled.

Dinner was ready, served out on the kitchen table.

" Call your father, Connie."

The old man came in, sat down at table and took up
his knife and fork. His plate was put in front of him,
and he began to eat at once. John's plate was filled
with food. His mother had given him the choicest of
everything. Connie looked at it and tittered " The Pro-
digal Son," she said. There was an awkward pause.
The old man looked angrily from side to side under his
heavy brows which, with his lowered head, gave him
the appearance of a bull swinging its head in wrath.

" I've told Vic. to come along, but he said he couldn't.
I think he might have done," said the mother com-
plainingly.

The four women kept jumping up, the two men sat
still to be waited on. Conversation was desultory, everyone took refuge in eating. At first John was hungry
but he was quickly satisfied. Yet the mountain on his
plate seemed hardly to decrease. His mother watched
his plate. " Is your potato all right, dear ?" she asked
and when she saw him flagging, " You must eat, son."
Her solicitude hung over him like an overwhelming
bosom. He knew that this dinner, this opportunity to
feed him, was the crux of the whole situation for her,
that she had been looking forward to it for weeks, that
every mouthful he took gave her pleasure. He struggled
on. It seemed as if he were not eating with his mouth
only, but absorbing food out of the laden air with his
whole body. The monstrous dishes bulged at him. Used
he to eat like this ? His stomach must have got pinched
lately. He got through the mountain somehow.

" I don't think I could manage any pudding, Mum,"
he said apologetically.

" Off your pecker ?" asked his father, staring at him.
" You wouldn't be any good in the carrying business."

His mother's face crinkled as if she were going to cry. Gwen stood on the other side of him, waiting, solicitious, sad. Connie stared at him with bright, malicious eyes.

" It's date pudding," his mother pleaded. "Your favourite pudding."

He owed her this even if only for that tranquil time in the kitchen. He wasn't going to do any of the other things she wanted, not marry Gwen, or seduce her, or come back home or give up any of his oddness. He'd have to do this for her. It was absurd, but it was real. He'd gone beyond her reach and she knew it. It was a cruel, open secret. All she could do for him now was mend his clothes and feed him when the opportunity offered. This was what her stored love had been waiting for.

" Oh, well, if it's DATE pudding. . . . I'll have some of that."

She brought him a big wedge. It had been boiled in a cloth, and had a damp, pale, outer rim. Yellow custard flowed round it. It was stiff with sweetness. It was like eating a pincushion.

" Gee, it's good," he said. A faint, pleased flush rose on his mother's cheek bones.

" Vic. ought to have come," she said. " Betty, don't feed him like this. Vic's. almost as fond of date pudding as you are. Have a little more, son, there's plenty out-side."

" No," he said firmly, " that would spoil it. What you gave me was just right."

" Now you lay down while we wash up," said his mother tenderly.

He was glad to. He lay on the hard couch in the drawing room because the one in the dining room was sacred to his father. He was aware of the absurdity of it. The two men lying down getting over their immense meals. It wouldn't be absurd to his father, only natural. He fell into a warm, sickly, half doze. Presently Gwen was sent in to entertain him. She chattered on and on, he could not even listen. His skin felt course and yellow, his mind leaden. The hours were like smooth, water-worn stones.

It was five o'clock. Down in the wooden office the telephone shrilled and shrilled. It was Gwen who went down to answer it, but only after they had argued as to whether it ought to be answered at all. She came back waving her arms. " It's for Jack," she called in the breathless voice that irritated him.

He hunched over the phone with a furtive air. The phone in the office always gave him that guilty feeling. It was a girl's voice with a slight nag in it. He stopped its flow.

" That'll be great, Coral. Of course you can count on me." He could not keep the relief out of his voice.

" Sounds as if I were rescuing you from the wilds of the family bosom."

He laughed to evade answering her, hating himself.

" I'll be with you in an hour."

" I can't promise you anything but a sardine and a biscuit."

He went back to the house. They raised enquiring faces.

" I've got to go back to town straight away." He didn't want to go, but, well, yes, it was a party of sorts, but he was going to see an editor there, a man who could help him. The words were dry in his mouth, he could hardly get them out.

His mother wailed, " I had such a nice tea for you."

" It's rotten luck," he mumbled. His one thought was to get away.

" I think you are hateful. Poor mother," said Connie in a low voice. There was no longer malice in her eyes, but contempt. The mother did not hear, she had gone out to the kitchen. John did not answer. What was the use when he would be gone in a few minutes ?

His mother came back with a cardboard box. She acquiesced in his going with the heavy resignation that she always showed her menfolk.

" I've put you up some things," she said. " Some tarts and cakes."

He took the box, distressed and wretched. He couldn't arrive at Coral's flat with the thing. He'd have to dump it somewhere. He kissed each of the women. Gwen's mouth flowered up softly under his. He felt himself caught in a web, silken, clinging. He put her aside roughly. The next moment he was running downhill towards the ferry, towards freedom, his shoulders hunched up, shabby, ungainly.

THE NEW DRESS

The first thing Mavis saw when she woke was the new dress hanging from the disused gas bracket. Her heart turned over with joy and she jumped out of bed to make sure that it was a fine day. By leaning out of the window and twisting her neck she could see a strip of sky, now the cool, bloomy blue of early morning. The air itself seemed conscious of a holiday and the very garbage tins in the lane below looked as if they were grouped for a still life. It was half past five, so there was still a long time to wait before she could put on the dress and go out to meet Lennie. Four hours, half a working day. She couldn't possibly sleep any more. All night she had slept lightly because she missed the anodyne of fatigue to which in the last two years her body had become accustomed. To go to bed not tired was from habit unsatisfactory. Without a weight against it the door of sleep kept flying open.

Even the milkman hadn't been, so she couldn't have a cup of tea. She sat on the bed, her chin on her drawn up knees, looking, in the skimpy cotton nightdress, much less than seventeen. The dress drew her thoughts like a magnet. It really was lovely, the loveliest, the first lovely thing, that she had had. Her glance caressed the full skirt, the shirred waist, the little close fitting bodice with its fischue collar, the bow of peach coloured velvet with long ends falling almost to the hem. But the colour was best of all. The printed silk showed a bright, rich confusion, damson coloured ovals slid over a background of peach with touches of rose and leaf green, and flecks of black, which gave the whole thing character. You wouldn't know it was only vegetable silk unless you were an expert. It was almost too good. She wouldn't mind just keeping it here and gloating over it.

Paying for the dress had been rather a struggle. She had made the first payment with the ten shillings Gran had sent her for her birthday. Then every week it had taken its toll. The money had had to come out somewhere, but she had never flinched. It was the waiting, not the scraping, that had gone hard with her. On Friday, rushing out in the tea break—they didn't get paid till the afternoon—she had triumphantly paid the last two instalments and got the frock out of the lay-by. This left her, after she had paid her rent and allowed enough for fares, the milkman and the baker, exactly one and eightpence. It was now only five days to pay day, and Lennie was paying everything today. That made four days. But over the head of the girl alone there always hangs the sword of emergencies.

Still she had the dress. That was everything. It had been crucial to have it for this week-end. She was going out for the day with Lennie, and then he was taking her home to have tea with his Auntie. Lennie had suggested this before, but Mavis had always found some excuse. Lennie, who like herself, had lost his parents, lived with his Auntie. She was a widow and owned the cottage they lived in. In Mavis's eyes such stability spelt wealth and the determination not to show herself before critical eyes until she could do Lennie credit was sunk like a caisson into her obstinate little heart. No dress, no Auntie. This, even though she knew that when a boy took his girl home it was almost as good as an understanding. And an understanding didn't fall far short of an engagement, which was, in Mavis's circle, the very pinnacle of achievement. Marriage itself was generally a retreat from glory into the struggle to make ends meet and bring up children on the hire purchase system.

The dress wasn't, except secondarily, for Lennie. Mavis knew that Lennie 'liked' her and that was quite enough for the present. Lennie was nice. He was a clerk in a city office. They had met at the roller skating and had taken a fancy to one another in the first five minutes.

Mavis worked at the perfumery counter in the bargain basement of a chain store. She liked it quite well though there were disadvantages like standing all day and not getting enough air to breathe. She thought the perfumery the best counter to be at, because most of the customers were girls like herself, hunting for a rainbow in the jungle.

She got on well with the other girls. There were two others in her sub-section, Gladys who was twenty and a ball of style, and Molly, fat, with a bad complexion and an all enveloping family life. Gladys was the leader. She knew the world.

Gladys approved of the dress, when Mavis took it out of its tissue paper in the dressing room on Friday night to exhibit it. She tried it against her own black curls and apricot skin with approbation, and she embellished the occasion with a lecture. "Don't let him put one over you, kiddy. You're just the soft sort they try it on." Someone had put it over Gladys a couple of years before and having come out on the other side she now felt that she knew all she needed to know about life. Mavis said no, she wouldn't, and wanted to get the dress back into its wrappings. It wasn't that sort of dress. It was for herself. It wasn't a lure, it was a protection. But she couldn't have said that any more than they could have understood it. It was a blind impulse dissolved in emotion.

Now it was time to dress, now it was time to go. But
the waiting for this long desired moment had been too
long, too empty. It had left its trace, a blank, flat spot
in the happy excitement of her mind.

The day was fine but heavy with heat, the sky of a
hazy blue that might turn to cloud, the light itself seemed
pigmented and fell on white walls with a coppery hue.
The city had a deserted, holiday look and already at
ten o'clock there were papers and other debris drifting
in the streets. Mavis and Lennie were going to Bobbin
Head. It meant first a train and then a bus. In the
electric train it was too noisy to talk but they smiled at
one another a lot. Everything was lovely except that
Lennie hadn't responded spontaneously to the new dress.
It was only in answer to a leading question that he said
it was very nice. They had what was to be the best
moment of the day in the crowded bus going out to the
picnic grounds. Pressed together in the crush they
looked at one another from a range of a few inches. They
felt intimate and alone. Mavis was sweet. Lennie was
nice. They shared a spurt of happiness.

They had lunch as soon as they arrived, although it
was early, because they were hungry. Auntie had prepared it for them—egg sandwiches, sausage rolls, fruit
and cake, with tea—tasting persistently of ink—in a
battered thermos.

Afterwards, Lennie suggested that they should go out
in a boat on the river but Mavis refused and he could
not persuade her. She wasn't going to risk the new dress
in a boat. This was a blow to Lennie, because as he had
planned the day over and over in his mind, and the boat
was an essential part. It would be cool on the water.
They could row for a bit, and then drift. They'd get out
of the crowd. He put it to Mavis all over again, but she

shook her head obstinately. What would they do? They couldn't sit here with children playing ball all over them. Would she come for a walk? Lennie knew that he wasn't being very pleasant about the change in his plans. He wanted to be magnaminous but he did feel sore.

" I don't want to get hot," said Mavis primly.

They started to walk towards the bushy slopes at the far side of the picnic ground, doggedly through the broiling midday sun, a couple of yards apart. The new dress was spoiling everything, Lennie thought sullenly. He thought it was hideous anyway, bright and ugly. It made Mavis look just like other girls, and she wasn't. And, worst of all, she'd put on a new manner with it. He was damned if he liked playing second fiddle to a bit of rag.

It wasn't much cooler in the bush, the trees cast little shade, the earth was parched and dusty. They walked on and on rather dolefully, looking for a place to sit. Whenever Lennie suggested a place Mavis said it was too sunny or too dusty. She was aware of dark moons of moisture staining the silk under her arms. She laddered her stocking on some prickly undergrowth, and was ready to cry. Then Lennie found quite a nice place down near the river with a fallen log in the shade. He spread his handkerchief on the ground and Mavis consented to sit on it, her back to the log. He sat beside her and tried to put his arm around her, but it was too hot and awkward. He took her little fist in his hand, tried to untwine the fingers, but when he felt her resistance he put it back in her lap. The dry earth ticked with little unseen insects. There was no other sound. The picnic ground was as far away as the sky.

They talked in a desultory way and presently Lennie lay down and put his head in her lap. She liked that. She pressed her fingers over his eyes and he smiled at her with his lips. This was better. The situation was knitting together. Lennie was content. If the chaps at the office could see him now they'd probably think him a terrible sissy. This wasn't their idea of spending a holiday, he could bet. They were rocked together in the cradle of the warm afternoon. They grew drowsy and did not resist. Soon they were asleep.

It may have been the thunder that woke them or the first drops of rain splashing on their faces. They woke simultaneously to a stormy light and a swish of advancing wind.

" We'd better get," said Lennie, jumping up and pulling Mavis after him by the hand. As they picked up their hats and the old suitcase they grinned rather sheepishly at each other. The joke was on them falling asleep like that, but they didn't mean to tell anyone.

They had nearly reached the edge of the bush before the rain caught them up. The trees offered little shelter, it was no good staying there to get wet. As they bolted across the open for the picnic sheds, it came down in a deluge. Every shelter was crowded already with boys and girls and family parties, but the nearest group made room cheerfully for Lennie and Mavis. Everyone was in crazy spirits and the rain had broken down all the taboos. The many separate picnics had become one large party. Stragglers were greeted with cheers, facetious advice and broad innuendoes. The wags were busy. Presently someone began to sing a popular song and the contagion spread from island to island, community singing in the rain. Lennie sang loudly, his arm round Mavis's shoulders, swinging her to the rhythm. Mavis was silent. She was wondering miserably what the rain had done to her dress. This worry made her feel very lonely. She twisted this way and that but could see nothing, they were all packed so tightly. She could only feel it, sodden against her legs.

It was not until they reached the railway station that she was able to assess the damage. The colours had run badly, and the skirt as it dried was shrinking. It was above her knees. It looked ridiculous and awful. It would never be the same. She looked at Lennie, her face hard with tragedy. He didn't know what to say in this purely feminine dilemma.

" It'll be all right when it's dry," he mumbled. She turned away. " Auntie'll iron it for you." As if that would be any good.

The train drew up and he bustled her in to get seats.

" I'm not going," she thrust at him as the train started.

" What ?"

" I'm not going."

" Not going where ?" he asked stupidly.

" To your Auntie's. I can't now."

He stared at her incredulously. " Why not ?"

" I couldn't possibly, looking like this."

" You look all right. Don't be a chump."

" I'm not going."

He knew that she meant it. He thought glumly of how he had dragooned his good natured, slatternly aunt into sprucing up the house, and of the tea she had promised to prepare for them.

" You can't let me down like this."

She shot him a glance that seemed to put all the blame on him. It couldn't only be the dress, she had been difficult all day.

He put his mouth to her ear in the rattling train.

" Did I do anything to upset you, Mavis ?"

" No."

" Are you angry with me ?"

She shook her head wearily. Why couldn't he leave her alone ?

" Look here," he said, " your beastly dress has spoiled our day. You were crazy to wear it to a picnic anyway. It serves you right."

At her look of anguish his anger died. He tried to put his arm round her. " Come home with me, lovie, Auntie and I have got everything so nice for you."

He didn't understand. The fiction supplements always said that men didn't understand, and it was quite true. It was no good offering her love in place of a spoiled dress.

She slumped down in her corner as far from him as she could get, and he sat looking out of the window, his face set, feeling more confused than angry. He'd never get the hang of Mavis. Girls were queer.

The week stretched miserably before Mavis. Four fourpenny lunches, a penny for the gas, and threepence for everything else. She wouldn't be able to go out, and Lennie wasn't likely to take her after this. Perhaps she'd never see him again. She'd put the dress between them and it had become a mountain. She wanted to say to him out of the new wisdom that was beginning to grow in her heart : " It has got to be like this now, but it will be all right soon. Be patient, Lennie, I'm not ready for you yet, but it won't be long now."

A few minutes later they parted in what looked like offended silence, but was only the natural confusion of their young hearts.

HABIT

Miss Jessle Biden was singing in a high plangent voice as she made the beds. It was a form of self-expression she allowed herself only when there were no guests in the house, and she mingled the hymns and sentimental songs of her girlhood with a fine impartiality. She made the beds with precision, drawing the much washed marcella quilts, with spikey fringes, up over the pillows so that the black iron bedsteads had an air of humility and self-respect. The sheets, though not fine, smelt amiably of grass, and the blankets were honest, if a little hard with much laundering. With the mosquito nets hanging from a hoop which in its turn, was suspended from a cup hook screwed into the wooden ceiling, the beds looked like virtuous but homely brides.

Jessie stopped singing for a minute as she pulled the green holland blind to the exact middle of the window, and surveyed the room to see if all were in order. She had very strict notions about the exact degree of circumspection to which paying guests were entitled. Yesterday everything washable in the rooms had been washed, the floor, the woodwork, the heavy florid china on the rather frail, varnished wooden washstands. The rooms smelled of soap, linoleum polish and wood. The lace curtains were stiff with starch. Indeed, there was more starch than curtain, and without it they would have been draggled and pitiful wisps.

As every door in the house was open and it was a light wooden shell of a place, old as Australian houses go, and dried by many summers, Jessie could quite comfortably talk to Catherine, who was cooking in the kitchen, from wherever she happened to be working. But presently, the rooms finished, she came to stand in the kitchen doorway with a list of the guests they were expecting for Easter, in her hand.

The kitchen was a pleasant room looking on to the old orchard, a row of persimmon trees heavy with pointed fruit turning golden in the early autumn, squat, round, guava bushes, their plump, red-coronetted fruit hidden in their glossy dark leaves, several plum and peach trees, one old wide-spreading apple tree and a breakwind of loquats and quinces. Beyond again was the bush, blue-green, shimmering a little in the morning sunshine.

Catherine Biden, too, was pleasant, and in keeping with the warm autumn landscape. Her red-gold hair, fine, heavy and straight, made a big bun on her plump white neck, her milky skin was impervious to the sun and her arms, on which her blue print sleeves were rolled up, were really beautiful. In the parlance of the neighbours, neither of the sisters would see forty again, which somehow sounded duller and more depressing than to say that Catherine was forty-two and Jessie forty-six.

" I'm putting the Adamses in the best room," Jessie was saying, " because they don't mind sharing a bed. And Miss Dickens and her friend in the room with the chest of drawers. Mrs. Holles says she must have a room to herself, so it will have to be the little one. The Thompsons and Miss George'll sleep on the verandah and dress together in the other room. The old lady and her niece next the dining room. That leaves only the verandah room this side, for Mr. Campbell."

" It's quite all right while the weather is cool," said Catherine, in her placid way, rolling dough.

Jessie looked at her list with disfavour. "We know everyone but Mr. Campbell. It's rather awkward having just one man and so many women."

" Perhaps he'll like it," Catherine suggested.

" I don't think so. His name's Angus. He's probably a man's man."

" Oh, if he's as Scotch as all that he won't mind. He'll fish all the time."

" Well, all I hope is he doesn't take fright and leave us with an empty room." The Easter season was so short, they couldn't afford an empty room.

" I hope," said Catherine, " we don't get a name for having only women. We do get more teachers every year and fewer men, don't we ?"

" Yes, we do. I think we'd better word the advertisement differently."

She sighed. Jessie, growing stout, with high cheek bones and a red skin, was the romantic one. She had always taken more kindly to this boarding house business than Catherine, because of its infinite possibilites—new people, new chances of excitement and romance. Although perhaps she no longer thought of romance, the habit of expecting something to happen remained with her.

Their father had married late. This house beside the lagoon had come to him with his wife and he had spent his long retirement in it, ministered to by his daughters. When he and his pension had died together, he had not, somehow, been able to leave them anything but the house, the small orchard and the lovely raggedy slope of wild garden running down to the water. Jessie, in a mood of tragic daring, advertised accommodation for holiday guests, carefully copying other advertisements she found in the paper. This expedient would, they hoped, tide them over. That was twelve years ago. A makeshift had become a permanency. In time, with the instrumentality of the local carpenter, they had added a couple of rooms and put up some almost paper-thin partitions. It looked as if they had developed the thing as far as they could.

They both still looked on their home as something different from their guest house. It was vested in that company of lares and penates now in bondage to mammon, but some day to be released. " Our good things," the sisters called them, the original furniture of the house, the bits and pieces that their mother had cherished. The big brass bed that had been their parents' was still in the best bedroom, though the cedar chest of drawers with pearl buttons sunk in its knobs and the marble topped washstand had gone to raise the tone of other rooms. The dining room was very much as it had always been. The sideboard with the mirrors and carved doors took up the best part of one wall, and set out on it was the old lady's brightly polished but now unused silver coffee service. The harmonium, with its faded puce silk, filled an inconvenient amount of room by the window. The old people's enlarged portraits, an ancient, elaborate worktable with dozens of little compartments, and other intimate treasures not meant for paying guests, but impossible to move out of their way, gave the room a genteel but overcrowded appearance. In the dining room in the off season it was almost as if nothing had ever happened.

In twelve years Jessie's hopefulness had worn a little thin and Catherine's gentle placid nature had become streaked with discontent, as marble is veined with black. Sometimes she asked herself where it was all leading, what would happen to them by and by and if this was all life had in store ? She began in a slow blind way to feel cheated, and to realise how meaningless was the pattern of the years with their alternations of rush and stagnation, of too much work and too little money. Of their darker pre-occupations the sisters did not speak to one another. In self defence they looked back rather than forward.

The guests began to arrive at lunch time. Angus Campbell was the last to come, by the late train, long after dark. Catherine went up to the bus stop with a lantern to meet him. He saw her for the first time with the light thrown upward on her broad fair face, and he thought how kind and simple and good she looked. His tired heart lifted, and he felt reassured.

Undressing in the small stuffy room they shared, next to the kitchen, Jessie asked her sister, " Do you think he'll fit in all right ?"

" I think so," Catherine answered. " He seems a nice, quiet man."

" Young ?" asked Jessie with the last flicker of interest in her tired body.

" About our age."

" Oh well . . . ."

They kissed one another good-night as they had every night since they were children, and lay down side by side to sleep.

The shell of a house was packed with sleeping people, all known and all strangers.

Angus Campbell evidently did not find his position of solitary man very trying, for on Easter Monday he asked, rather diffidently, if he might stay another week. He was taking his annual holidays. When the other guests departed, he remained. One week grew into two, then he had to return to Sydney.

He was a tall, gaunt, slightly stooped man with a weather-beaten complexion—the kind of Scots com-

plexion that manages to look weather beaten even in a
city office—and a pair of clear, understanding, friendly,
hazel eyes. His manner was very quiet and at first he
seemed rather a negligible and uninteresting man. But
presently you discovered in him a steadfast quality that
was very likeable. You missed him when he went away.

When he was alone with the sisters, life settled inevitably into a more intimate rhythm. They ate their
meals together on a rickety table on the verandah, where
they could look over the garden to the lagoon. He
would not let the sisters chop wood or do the heavy
outdoor work that they were accustomed to, and he even
came into the kitchen and helped Jessie wash up while
Catherine put away. He did it so simply and naturally
that it seemed right and natural to them.

One day he began digging in the garden, and, from
taking up the potatoes they wanted, went on to other
things. " You oughtn't to be doing this," Jessie said.
" It's your holiday."

" You don't know how I enjoy it," he answered, and
his eyes, travelling over the upturned loamy earth to the
blazing persimmon trees and the bush beyond, had in
them a look of love and longing. She knew that he
spoke the truth.

He went out fishing and brought back strings of fish
for their supper with pride and gusto, and then had to
watch Catherine cook them. There seemed to be something special about Catherine cooking the fish he caught.

He helped Catherine pick fruit for jam and she was
aware that for all he was thin and stooped he was much
stronger than she, and it gave her a curious, pleased
feeling. Jessie, alone in the house, could hear their voices
in the orchard, a little rarefied and idealised, in the still
warm air.

One day it rained, great gusts of thick fine rain that blotted out the lagoon, and Angus, kept in, took his book on to the verandah. Passing to and fro doing the work, Cartherine saw that he was not reading, but looking out into the rain. Then he went and stood by the verandah rail for a long time. She came and stood beside him.

He said, " If you listen you can just hear the rain on the grass and among the leaves—and smell the earth. It's good, isn't it ? The trees are more beautiful looming through the mist—the shape of them." Marvelling, she saw that he was half in love with the beauty that she had lived with all her life.

A magpie flew through the rain, calling. He laid his hand on her shoulder and she was a little shaken by that warm and friendly touch. The eyes he turned on her still held the reflection of a mystery she had not seen.

Angus Campbell told them about himself. He was a clerk in a secure job and for years he had looked after his invalid mother, coming home from the office to sit with her, getting up in the night to tend her, his money going in doctor's bills. She had often been querulous and exacting. " The pain and the tedium were so hard for her to bear, and there was so little I could do for her. Of course I remember her very different. No one could have had a better mother. She was very ambitious for me, and made great sacrifices when I was a boy, so that I should have a good education and get on. But I never did—not very far." It was evident that he thought he owed her something for that disappointment. Two months ago she had died and he missed her bitterly. " She had become my child," he said. He felt, too, the cruelty of her life that had been hard and unsatisfied, and had ended in pain. Now there was no hope of ever retrieving it.

" He is very good," said Jessie to her sister when they were alone that night.

" And kind," said Catherine. " The kindest man I've ever known."

Neither of them thought how few men they'd known.

Jessie raised herself on her elbow to look at Catherine as she slept in the faint moonlight, and thought how comely she was, sweet and wholesome.

When Angus had, at last, to go, he said he would be back for the week-end. They kissed him. He was to arrive on the Friday by the late train again, and Catherine prepared supper for him before the fire, for it was getting cold now. She took the silver coffee pot, the sacred silver coffee pot that had been their mother's, and put it to warm above the kitchen stove. She cast a half defiant glance at Jessie as she did so, but Jessie went and took the silver sugar bowl too, and the cream jug, filled them, and set them on the table.

Angus asked Catherine to go out in the boat with him or to go walking, and then he paid Jessie some little attention. But they both knew. One Sunday, perhaps it was the fourth week-end he had come, the autumn was now far advanced, he and Catherine went for a long walk and he asked her to marry him. He took her in his arms and kissed her. She felt very strange, for she had never been kissed before, not by a man who was in love with her. They walked home hand in hand as if they were still very young, and when Catherine saw Jessie waving to them from the verandah she stood still and the unaccountable tears began to flow down her cheeks.

They said, everybody said, that there was no reason why they should wait, meaning they had better hurry up. The wedding was fixed for three months ahead,

It was a curious three months for Catherine. When Angus came for the week-end they would not let him pay his board, and that made a little awkwardness. Even calling him Angus seemed a trifle strange. He did not come every week-end now. Once he said, " It seems wrong to take you away from all this beauty and freedom and shut you up in a little suburban house among a lot of other little houses just the same. Do you think you'll fret, my darling ?"

Catherine had never thought very much about the beauties of nature. So she just shook her head where it rested against his shoulder. Still, her heart sank a little when she saw his house with its small windows, dark stuff hangings and many souvenirs of the late Mrs. Campbell. It seemed as if sickness and death had not yet been exorcised from it.

Catherine and Jessie sewed the trousseau. "We must be sensible," they said to one another, and bought good stout cambric and flannelettes, though each secretly hankered after the pretty and the foolish. Catherine could not quite forget that she was going to be a middle aged bride, and that that was just a little ridiculous. Neighbours, meaning to be kind, teased her about her wedding and were coy, sly and romantic in a heavy way, so that she felt abashed.

A subtle difference had taken place in the relationship of the sisters. Jessie felt a new tenderness for Catherine. She was the younger sister who was going to be married. Jessie's heart burned with love and protectiveness. She longed, she didn't know why, to protect Catherine, to do things for her. " Leave that to me," she would say when she saw Catherine go to clean the stove or perform some other dirty job. " You must take care of your hands now."

But Catherine always insisted on doing the roughest work. " He's not marrying me for my beauty," she laughed.

Catherine too thought more of her sister and of how good and unselfish she was, and her little peculiarities that once rather irritated her, now almost brought the tears to her eyes. One night she broached what was always on her mind.

" What will you do when I've gone ?" she asked in a low voice.

"·I'll get Ivy Thomas to help me in the busy times," Jessie answered in a matter of fact voice, " and in between, I'll manage."

" But it will be lonely," said Catherine weakly.

Jessie cast a reproachful glance at her. "I'll manage," she said.

Catherine was no longer discontented and weighed down with a sense of futility. Another emotion had taken its place, something very like homesickness.

As she did her jobs about the place she thought now, " It is for the last time," and there was a little pain about her heart. She looked at her world with new eyes. Angus's eyes perhaps. Going down to the fowlyard in the early morning with the bucket of steaming bran and pollard mash, she would look at the misty trees and the water like blue silk under the milk-pale sky ; at the burning autumn colours of the persimmon trees, and the delicate frosty grass, and her heart would tremble with its loveliness.

One evening, coming in with the last basket of plums —ripe damsons with a thick blue bloom upon them— she stopped to rest, her back to the stormy sunset, and she saw thin, blue smoke like tulle winding among the quiet trees where a neighbour was burning leaves. She thought that she would remember this all her life. Picking nasturtiums under the old apple tree she laid her cheek for a moment against the rough silvery bark, and closed her eyes. " My beloved old friend," she thought but without words, " I am leaving you for a man I scarcely know."

It would seem as if the exaltation of being loved, of that one ripe and golden Sunday when she thought she could love too, had become detached from its object and centred now about her home. She even became aware of a rhythm in her daily work. Objects were dear because her hands were accustomed to them from childhood. And now life had to be imagined without them.

" Wherever I am, I shall have to grow old," she she thought, " and it would be better to grow old here where everything is kind and open, than in a strange place." It was as if the bogey she had feared, meaningless old age, had revealed itself a friend at the last moment, too late.

Jessie lit the porcelain lamp with the green shade and set it in the middle of the table among the litter of the sewing. She stood adjusting the wick, her face in shadow, and said :

" We'll have to have a serious talk about the silver and things, Cathy. We'd better settle it to-night before we get too busy."

" What about them ?" Catherine asked, biting off a thread.

" You must have your share. We'll have to divide them between us." Jessie's voice was quite steady and her tone matter of fact.

" Oh, no," cried Catherine, with a sharp note of passion in her voice. " I don't want to take anything away."

" They are as much yours as mine."

" They belong here."

" They belong to both of us, and I'm not going to have you go away empty handed."

" But, Jessie, I'll come back often. The house wouldn't seem the same without mother's things. Don't talk as if I were going away for ever."

" Of course you'll come back, but it won't be the same. You'll have a house of your own."

" It won't be the same," echoed Catherine very low.

" I specially want you to have mother's rings. I've always wanted you to wear them. You've got such pretty hands and now you won't have to work so hard. . . . and the pendant. Father gave that to mother for a wedding present so as you're the one getting married it is only fit you should wear it on your wedding day too. I'll have the cameos. I'm sort of used to them. And the cat's eye brooch that I always thought we ought to have given Cousin Ella when mother died." Jessie drew a rather difficult breath.

" You're robbing yourself," said Catherine, " giving me all the best. You're the eldest daughter."

" That has nothing to do with it. We must think of what is suitable. I think you ought to have the silver coffee things. They've seemed specially yours since that night—you remember—when Angus came. Perhaps they helped . . . ."

Catherine made a funny little noise.

" I don't want the silver coffee set."

" Yes, you do. They're heeps too fine for guests. They're good. What fair puzzles me is the work table. You ought to have it because after all I suppose I'll be keeping all the big furniture, but this room wouldn't be the same without it."

" No," cried Catherine. "Oh, Jessie, no. Not the work table. I couldn't bear it." And she put her head down among the white madapolam and began to cry, a wild, desperate weeping.

" Cathy, darling, what is it ? Hush, Petie, hush. We'll do everything just as you want."

" I won't strip our home. I won't."

" No, darling, no, but you'll want some of your own friendly things with you."

Jessie was crying a little too, but not wildly. " You're overwrought and tired. I've let you do too much." Her heart was painfully full of tenderness for her sister.

Catherine's sobs grew less at last, and she said in a little gasping, exhausted voice. " I can't do it."

" I won't make you. It can stay here in its old place and you can see it when you come on a visit."

" I mean I can't get marired and go away. It's harder than anything is worth."

Jessie was agast. They argued long and confusedly. Once Catherine said : " I wish it had been you, Jessie."

Jessie drew away. " You don't think that I . . . ."

" No, dear, only on general grounds. You'd have made such a good wife and," with a painful little smile, " you were always the romantic one."

" Not now," said Jessie staunchly.

" I'll write to Angus now, tonight," Catherine declared.

She wanted to be rid of this intolerable burden at once, although Jessie begged her to sleep on it. Neither of them had considered Angus, nor did they now. She got out the bottle of ink, and the pen with the cherry wood handle, which they shared, and began the letter. She was stiff and inarticulate on paper, and couldn't hope to make him understand. It was a miserable, hopeless task but she had to go through with it.

While she bent over the letter, Jessie went out into the kitchen and relit the fire. She took the silver coffee pot, the sugar basin and the cream jug, and set them out on the tray with the best worked traycloth. From the cake tin she selected the fairest of the little cakes that had been made for the afternoon tea of guests arriving tomorrow. Stinting nothing, she prepared their supper. When she heard Catherine sealing the letter, thumping the flap down with her fist to make the cheap gum stick, she carried in the tray.

Although she felt sick with crying, Catherine drank her coffee and ate a cake. The sisters smiled at one another with shaking lips and stiff redened eyelids.

"He won't come again now," said Jessie regretfully, but each added in her heart, "He was a stranger, after all."

THE DRESSMAKER

Miss Simkins arrived early at the Bowker's to do her day's sewing. She had to come early because, of course, everyone wanted their full eight hours, and liked her to be well out of the way and the house tidied up before their menfolk came home in the evening. It was just half-past eight when she open the Bowker's gate, and there was Mrs. Bowker waiting for her on the verandah. " Why, Miss Simkins," she called, " I thought you had missed the train. I've everything ready."

The kitchen table had been carried out on to the glassed-in verandah, the machine was open, the work-basket beside it. Mrs. Bowker made rather a merit of being punctual, and having everything ready. This stuck a little in Miss Simkins' throat, because Mrs. Bowker certainly profited by her punctuality, in that it wrung the maximum of labour out of Miss Simkins. Therefore the merit, if any, was hers and not Mrs. Bowkers'. It was Mrs. Bowker who received, and she who gave, and yet Mrs. Bowker always said " I've everything ready for you," as if she had prepared a special treat.

Miss Simkins did not see very much of life but what she saw she inspected very closely and she kept an exact debit and credit account between herself and life. She always observed her employers' conduct and utterences minutely with a view to keeping this statement up-to-date. She was, she felt, one of life's principal creditors.

These thoughts were habitual, automatic, and, of course, unvoiced. She merely took off her hat, which collapsed into immediate shapelessness, gave two pokes to her hair and sat down to the work-table. From her suitcase she produced a sheaf of battered fashion journals.

" Edna," called Mrs. Bowker. " Edna !" Her voice shot up like a jack-in-the-box, surprisingly shrill for her comfortable bulk. " You'd better get on with the school tunic for Joyce, while Miss Bowker and I look at the patterns," she said.

Edna Bowker came in, a tall, slight girl, with very red hair and a very white skin, a very small mouth and very large eyes. She had a lanquid air as if even her eyelashes were a burden. (A young man had told her that she was like a hesitation waltz, so she acquired the habit of hesitating more and more even in the morning.)

" Good morning, Miss Simkins," she said politely.

A little warmth crept into the cold, glassy room. A faint excitement beat up from the fashion books. Miss Simkins cut boldly into the blue serge, making cold metallic noises with the scissors, and putting pins in her mouth. " It's all collars and sleeves this year," she announced through them.

" I don't like them too exaggerated," said Mrs. Bowker.

" Miss Bowker has a long neck. She can stand it."

" She's got the fashionable figure. I'll say that for her."

" She has so."

" I'm too thin," announced Edna. " I'd do anything to put on weight, but I can't."

" Oh, would she ?" thought Miss Simkins.

" There's a pretty one on page 6. I made it for a client at Strathfield last week. She was delighted with it. Very wealthy people."

" That's the one I like."

" But it's too old for you."

" Oh, no, mother, I look simply poisonous in girlish clothes. It's my height."

" But you needn't look as if you were thirty. Need she, Miss Simkins ?"

" My gracious, no."

" I know what I want, Mother."

" She has always known what she wanted ever since she was a baby. The thing is, is there enough stuff ? I got five yards."

" Well, five yards would be very bare. Um—yes those sleeves do cut into it. I'd have to have some joins."

" I hate joins," said Edna, passionately.

" You could have the collar and different sleeves."

" I suppose you haven't got 'Vogue' ?"

" Well, no, Miss Bowker. I don't get 'Vogue'. You wouldn't believe how much those books cost."

" I do think 'Vogue' is so chick."

She looked intently at the illustrations. Would she really look like that if Miss Simkins copied the dress ? She was always filled with an agony of hope when the dressmaker came, but she had never got exactly what she wanted. Not exactly.

" If," she said dreamily, " I could only have a little feather hat like that."

" We might see," said Mrs. Bowker. " We'll price them. Mr. Bowker," she explained, " thinks the world of his girlies. He likes them to look their best. What I say to him is, he won't have the privilege of buying their clothes for long. Edna's as good as engaged now."

" Mother," cried Edna, " you shouldn't say that, there's nothing fixed."

" I only said 'as good as'." Edna plunged down among the fashion books. She tried not to hear her mother. She couldn't imagine why she felt so uncomfortable.

Mrs Bowker lowered her voice, presumably that the spirit of romance, now hovering over the house, might not take fright. " Such a nice young fellow. He'll have plenty by and bye. He's got his car and all that now."

" How nice," said Miss Simkins.

" Edna's had plenty of chances, but this time it's serious. Alan is mad about her. Everybody has noticed it. So you see we want to make a special effort with her clothes."

Miss Simkins saw perfectly. She bit off a length of cotton.

The maid brought in morning tea. " I think morning tea is a mistake," said Mrs. Bowker. " It spoils lunch." Miss Simkins couldn't help hoping there would be something worth spoiling. Her early breakfast had been a very ghostly affair. For the present there was thin captain biscuits, buttered but rather soft.

" Do mind the butter," cried Mrs. Bowker in an agony of anxiety.

Edna wandered out into the kitchern and returned with a slice of cake in one hand, and a tart in the other. " I'm always eating," she said, laughing it off.

The machine whirred, Mrs. Bowker ran in tackings, Edna still sat hunched over the fashion books. She was looking at wedding dresses, and her lips moved as if she were telling herself a story. " There's some finishing you can do, Edna," said her mother. " U-um—half minute," answered the girl.

Miss Simkins was turning the Bowkers over in her private mind. She supposed they were a happy family. They all thought a lot of one another. But she really couldn't see why. They weren't very exciting, were they? She had seen Mr. Bowker. He had a brick red face and very thick, red eyebrows. She supposed Mrs. Bowker had been romantic about him once. Edna's young man they were so pleased about, was probably ordinary too.

Really, some people got everything very easily. It didn't matter a bit that Mrs. Bowker was stout and stupid and rather mean too, or that Edna was spoilt and affected, or that everything about them was utterly, overwhelmingly commonplace. They had one another, they had Mr. Bowker, a man, to fend for them. It made all the difference.

Mrs. Bowker went on talking. " My son says. . . . My husband. . . . Our girlies. . . . Edna . . . . Joycie. . . . My son . . . . My hubbie . . . ." It wasn't necessary to listen. Miss Simkins knew all that—from the outside.

Then it was lunch time. Miss Simkins gave two pokes to her hair, shook the cottons from her skirt, and they went into the cold, rather dark, dining-room. Miss Simkins looked round the table and her heart sank. It was corned beef and carrots. Miss Simkins had noticed that it was always either corned beef or sausages—never a roast or fillet steak or boiled chicken or fried sole—but it was a mistake to think of these things for they made the corned beef, with its rind of thick, yellow fat and its mottled, brownish flesh, (bought ready cooked at the smallgoods shop, she knew) and the hot carrots, smelling of earth, lying beside the cold meat on the warm plate, seem even more unappetising than it was. People must think that dressmakers liked corned beef and sausages above everything else. No, it wasn't that. People didn't think at all, that was the hardest part to bear.

Edna, it appeared, was not going to have corned beef. She had a chop instead. She explained that it was left over from last night, and it would be a pity to waste it. It did not look at all left over, but was fresh and juicy with a rich gravy mottling the plate. It smelt most appetising too, and when Edna put a lump of butter on top of it, peppering it well, that chop fairly took hold of Miss Simkins' imagination.

Neither, it turned out, was Mrs. Bowker going to have corned beef. She never took meat more than once a day, and they were having a nice little stuffed shoulder for dinner. The corned beef, it was obvious, had been bought entirely for Miss Simkins—a quarter of a pound. Mrs. Bowker had lettuce, and cheese, and brown bread, and some stewed apple with the cream off the milk. She needed, she said, something nourishing, she ate so little. They ought to be glad they had their appetites. Edna said mother ate nothing, and she was glad Miss Simkins was there because often she felt such a beast, eating a hearty lunch while mother just pecked. Mrs. Bowker's delicacy did not show, however, unless it was in her habit of looking intently, and rather suspiciously at every piece of food before she took it on her plate.

Miss Simkins' heart rebelled against the corned beef. She longed to say that she didn't eat it, but she was hungry, and there did not appear to be anything else. Besides, it would be rude. Mrs. Bowker would probably remember it against her, and not send for her again. She put a small piece of meat in her mouth. It lay cold and dead on her tongue. It seemed utterly alien. It was very stupid and very gross to feel so keenly about food. But she did. She could have wept.

Lunch over, Miss Simkins felt more cheerful, despite herself. Also the sun had reached the glassed-in verandah and it was now bright and pleasant. The warmth brought a familiar, friendly, oily smell out of the sewing machine and the light was better. Edna had a fitting. She disliked being fitted, because Miss Simkins had cold hard fingers, and because she stood so close that she could feel her breath on her neck, her bare arms, her cheek.

She could see Miss Simkins' scalp, greyish white, through her course, dun-coloured hair. She could see the enlarged pores on her nose and she hated it. She hated having anybody touch her, except her own people—or Allan. She stood like a dummy while her mother and Miss Simkins argued over the dress.

" Well, Mrs. Bowker, that was how we always did it at Summerhayes in London—on the right side. You'll see when it's finished it'll look all right. M. Pitot would have taken a fit if anyone had done it different. They never do in France."

Mrs. Bowker was impressed. Even she had heard of Summerhayes in London.

" Well," she said, " I suppose you know, Miss Simkins. Only I was taught different. Not that I'm much of a hand at sewing. With four children, one has just to do the best one can and do it quickly. I never knew you were at Summerhayes."

" Why, yes, Mrs. Bowker, I had a very good position there. I was with them for ten years, and I rose to be head of one of the rooms. Not the fitting, that was M. Pitot. I used to do all the trimming and finishing, and dresses were trimmed in those days—before the war."

" Fancy," said Mrs. Bowker, and, after a pause : " I wonder you left it to come out here."

" I never thought I'd come to dressmaking by the day, I never did. You see I left to get married. I had a great disappointment. I think you can take it off now, Miss Bowker. Mind the pins. It was all very strange how it came about. More like a novel than real life, I always say. My romance, I mean."

Miss Simkins laughed self-consciously, and Mrs. Bowker said " Fan·cy," again.

" I was at Summerhayes and I used to take my fortnight's holiday in August. This particular August I went
away with another of the young ladies to a place in
Norfolk. We used to go boating on the Broads with a
gentleman acquaintance we made, and one day we had
an accident. There was a boat coming towards us with
several young men in it, and one of them played the fool,
and well—somehow or other they ran into us and we
capsized. I couldn't swim a stroke and I really think I
would have been drowned if one of the strange young
gentlemen hadn't jumped in and rescued me. I was wet
through, of course, and rather frightened. Dear, he was
in a way about me. He put his coat round me and rowed
me to the landing stage as fast as he could. Then he got
a cab and took me and my friend home. You wouldn't
believe how handsome he looked with his wet hair plast-
tered to his forehead, and his shirt clinging to his broad
shoulders. He came the next day to see how I was, and
the day after that. And then we started going out for
walks together, and I hardly saw anything of my friend
for the rest of the holiday. She was quite snappy about
it, I remember."

" Excuse me, Miss Simkins, but you won't forget
we're having the collar two inches wider than the pattern ?"

" No, I haven't forgotten, Mrs. Bowker—this is the
cuff. I went back to London and so did he. He was in
an office not far away from the shop and we saw one another a lot. He was mad about me, Mrs. Bowker."

" It's too like a book," thought Edna. " I don't believe it."

" It seems he didn't like being in an office, and he had
great ideas of coming out to Australia and farming. He
had some money, but his people didn't like the idea of

him leaving England. Well, I backed him up. There
are too many clerks in London. It was up to him to do
more with his life than that. I do believe in ambition,
don't you, Mrs. Bowker ?"

" Why, yes. I always say to my boy. . . . ."

But this was Miss Simkins' hour, she swept on. " Arthur
thought a lot of my judgment. He said if I'd marry him
he'd be ready for anything. So we were engaged, and he
took me to see his mother and sister but they were very
stiff with me. You see, they thought I was stealing
Arthur and influencing him to leave England. I was all
for marrying and coming out with Arthur, but he said
no, he'd have a home for me first. He wasn't going to
have me roughing it. He was a very chivalrous nature
and he couldn't bear me to have so much as a finger ache."

" No, Elaine," he said, " I'll have to earn you first."
(" My name's Elaine. My mother was very romantic.
The Lily Maid of Astolat, you know.")

Edna couldn't help looking at the mole on Miss Simkins' chin, with its little fountain of hairs.

" After a year Arthur wrote for me to come. He was
doing better than he expected, and had a little home
ready for me. His property was out from Goulburn,
very good land, and he'd had a good season. (I had all
my linen ready and a lot of other things.) I spent all my
savings on an outfit and things for the house, and Summerhayes' gave me my wedding dress. M. Pitot designed it
himself, so you see what they thought of me."

" My," said Mrs. Bowker politely.

" At Melbourne there was a wire for me, but when I
got to Sydney, no Arthur. I didn't know what to do,
and while I was waiting on the boat hoping he'd come,
I got a telegram from the matron of the hospital at
Goulburn to say Arthur was there and had met with an

accident. I caught the train that night and arrived in the early hours of the morning. I found my poor lad very ill. It was all on account of me he'd been hurt, for he was so anxious to have everything ready for me that he worked on into the night, tidying up the place. In the dark he stumbled on an axe and it cut deep into his leg. There was no one to help him, and he would have bled to death if he hadn't managed to tie up the artery some-how. By morning his leg was in such a state he could not move it. The neighbour, who had promised to feed his horse while he was away, came over two days later— the day he was to have come to Sydney for me—and found him delirious, with his leg black and swollen. He hurried him to hospital, and the matron wired me.

" Arthur was terribly changed. His face looked small like a child's, and his eyes, two black pits in it. They had to amputate his poor leg, but that didn't do him any good. He wasted and wasted. They were kind to me at the hospital, and let me stay with him. (He wanted so much to get better, and even when he was at his worst he knew me.) One day he said, " I want to make my will, Ellie. Will you get me a lawyer ?" But I laughed and said, " Plenty of time for that. You'll only have to make another as soon as you're married." I didn't want him to think he was dying, you see. He didn't ask again, and that afternoon he said he was feeling better and had less pain, but in the night, at two o'clock, he died."

Miss Simkins was sitting quite still with her hands in her lap, looking out of the window. Edna felt terribly uncomfortable. Mrs. Bowker was embarrassed too, and thought she really ought to suggest that Miss Simkins went on with her work.

" I was very ill with grief and shock myself then, and when I got better I'd no money left, and no claim on anything of Arthur's. His mother thought if it hadn't been for me he'd have been alive still, so she had the land and our little house sold and didn't give me anything."

Miss Simkins fell to machining again. Mrs. Bowker and Edna looked at one another.

· · · · · · · ·

The dress was finished and Miss Simkins had gone before Joyce came home from school. She was a fair, leggy girl, full of vitality and curiosity. Even the advent of the dressmaker seemed to her an incident out of which some excitement could be squeezed. She began to pester her mother with questions. " How did Miss Simkins get on ? Did she bring some nice fashion books ? Did she have any news ?"

" Well, she talked a lot," said Mrs. Bowker.

" What did she say ? What did she say ?" cried Joyce, jumping up and down.

" She told us the story of her life," answered Mrs. Bowker, beginning to smile.

" Did she have an exciting life ?"

" I'm afraid not."

" What happened ?"

" The usual thing," Edna cut in. " She nearly got married, but not quite."

" She talks too much," said Mrs. Bowker. " I don't think we can have her again."

· · · · · · · ·

Miss Simkins went home happy. Always when she had told her story she had a sense of exaltation. She had had romance, even if she hadn't been able to keep it.

She couldn't help thinking that there was something fine about her tragedy. It was more beautiful than the commonplace happiness of mediocre people.

Tonight she was going to give herself a little treat. She bought a portion of steamed chicken, a paper bag of potato crisps, a punnet of strawberries, and a little carton of mixed nuts.

" Why not ?' she asked herself, defiantly.

DRY SPELL

I walked because there was no reason for stopping, because it was more intolerable to stay still, and because I wanted to reach the sea. I wanted to wade out into the water and perform some ritual act—like the Doge wedding Venice to the Adriatic, or William the Conqueror with his hands full of symbolic mud, or Cuchulain, or McDouall Stuart rushing into the Indian Ocean when he had crossed the continent, or Cortes greeting the Pacific—but was that Pisarro, or was it somebody else altogether, Drake perhaps ? My mind caught painfully on the doubt like a plane running on a knot of hardwood. It upset me. I began rubbing my hand across my chin again, and listening to my footsteps. The things I had not been thinking came closer.

I was coming into the city along Anzac Parade. It was late and quiet. Occasionally a tram passed, an empty, illuminated box, leaping on the rails under a crackle of blue sparks. The trees were black, and their leaves made a little dry sound like ghostly butter pats. There were no soft, rounded, sounds in the night, only dry brittle ones, and the pavement was gritty under my feet. My lips tasted of dust as they always did. The torrid street lamps were like sores on the night.

Walking alone at night always stimulated my imagination and now I was exalted as if with fever. But it was the city's fever, not mine. Images, like the empty, lit tram, ran through my mind and I was aware, with a febrile intensity, of my surroundings, immediate and remote.

It was the third waterless summer, and the heat had come down like a steel shutter over the city. The winters between had been as bad. Dry, with a parching, un-slacked cold ; westerly winds that drove and drove, bringing such clarity to the air, that a hill five miles away looked near enough to touch. The drought was in everything now, penetrating and changing life like blind roots at work upon a neglected pavement. The colours and quality of the world had been altered in the long months of desiccation. The pattern of existence was pulled awry.

Around the city there was a great fan of desolation. The sun had beaten the Emu Plains to a black brown on which the isolated houses and the townships themselves drifted like flotsam on a dead sea. The mountains were not blue but purple, a waterless ridge of rocks and shadows with the vegetation, except in the deepest seams of the valleys, mummified and black. Beyond again the Bathurst Plains were like a petrified sea, and very quiet. Further west, in an eternity of their own, were the iron-hard, fissured Black Soil Plains. There was no green anywhere. The stock had been driven away to agistment over the border long ago. Or had died. There was nothing even for the crows, who last year had had their saturnalia.

The country with its endless, aching death pressed in on the city, the drought and the heat pressed on both. In the city and its environs its stamp was no less clear. The bush on the outskirts was more than half dead. Even the deep feeders, the black butts and the like, were dying. The life that was left was drawn in and banked down, muted and secret. The scrub was shabby and colourless. Fire had licked through it, leaving patches of black and sharp red-brown. Where there were houses, wide fire breaks had been cut as the only protection. Water could no longer be relied on to combat the fires.

These breaks were raw scars, even on the devastated
country. They looked like the trail of vengeance. Orchards
were long since dead, and the trees fallen on the eroded
ground. On the eastern slopes around Dural the orange
trees were burnt black. The flats that used to be vegetable gardens were bare, the last dried stalks blown
away. Even Chinamen could make nothing grow.

In the wealthy suburbs of the North Shore and Vaucluse
a change had taken place too. It was as if the earth had
been squeezed so that all the fine houses that had nestled
so comfortably in the contours and in the greenery,
were forced up into the light. They bulged out, exposed,
and the sun tore at them. The gardens that had em-
bowered them were perished. Tinder dry, fire had been
through many of them, scorching walls and blistering
away any paint that remained. Most of these houses
were empty or inhabited as if they were caves, by people
who had come in from the stricken country. The owners
had fled, not so much from present hardship, as from the
nebulous threat of the future, the sense of being trapped
in a doomed city. The shores of the harbour were lion-
coloured or drab grey. Sandhills showed a vivid whiteness.
Only the water was alive and brilliant. And it was salt.

In the crowded districts, there was less to perish, but
light and air were equally abrasive, changing all surfaces,
fading and nullifying all colour. There was no pleasure
of touch left anywhere, for the dust was undefeatable.
It pulled down pride and effort. The suburbs sagged
under an intolerable burden.

I was perpetually aware of all this. It cumulated into
a black wave which hung over me in threatening suspense.
Nothing that I knew had escaped. From my windows I
looked over the golf course and that had taken, because
it was defenceless, the clearest print of all. Its silvery

green hills were stripped to pale brown and tawny purple. The earth was like starved, sagging flesh on an iron skeleton. Here and there a fire had run for a few yards before it died for lack of tinder, and left a black smear with a little edging of white ash. I used to think that the desert of Arizona looked like that. Now I know that heat and drought can bring even the gentlest country to it.

There was a man walking in front of me that I hadn't noticed before. When he passed a lamp I saw that he was a different shape from the pedestrians you'd expect to see about there. He was a swaggie all right with his roll of old blue blanket across his shoulders, and his quart pot dangling from it. I overhauled him.

" Good-night, mate."

" 'Night, mate," he answered, as a bushman answers the gate-crashing townsman. He was an old-timer, might have been a fossicker, short and spare, with a wealth of grey whiskers and clothes subdued to use and wont as only a bushman's can be.

" Come far?" I asked him.

" Middlin' far."

" Where's that ?" I felt an insatiable curiosity.

" Back o' beyond."

I'd seen hundreds like him but here there was a sort of long range persistance that was impressive. His gaunt and bristling dog at heel was cut out of the same stuff. My imagination took a leap.

" Did you ever do a perish on the Diamantina ?"

" Aye, there and more places besides."

" And now the track runs through the city?"

He didn't answer. So that was the way of it. I felt coldly sick. Looking back over my shoulder I saw that there were others, many of them, moving singly among the trees, all with the same intent, converging, persistance. It would be the same on all the other highways. I took to the middle of the road and, almost, to my heels.

I reached Taylor Square ahead of them. The neon signs were sizzling, and a few shop windows still bulged with light on the indifferent night. There were hardly any people about, but in the narrow, crowded streets at the bottom of the hill there were plenty, sitting on door steps or on chairs dragged out on to the pavement. Children were playing languidly in the street because it was too hot to go to bed. There was a queue at the pump, with buckets and kerosene tins and even jugs.

There was still water in the pipes, brownish stuff with a smell, but the pressure was so poor that it didn't reach the higher levels, so the pumps had been put in where people could come and get it. The city hadn't been used to queues, and they were changing peoples' outlook. They made new channels for rumour, perhaps for thought.

So many things were different, and the men's minds with them. Unemployment was general either directly from scarcity, or from its by-product of apathy. Idleness was everywhere and the people were differently distributed. Whole districts were almost depopulated whilst others were overcrowded to suffocation. Practically all the food had to be brought in. The Government was distributing it as a ration. There was enough, and yet it didn't slake the public appetite. There was a sense of famine. Even those who were eating better than ever before, felt it. The whole of our civilization was piled up like a pyre waiting for the fire to consume it.

The city seethed with rumours and with the promulgators of fantastic schemes, but everyone was fatalistic about the drought. They didn't expect it to break, they even took an inverted pride in it. It, at least, relieved them of the responsibility of living their own lives. There was always a crowd at the General Post Office reading the bulletins that were posted hourly, but no one believed the jargon of lows, depressions and tropical disturbances, any more than they believed in the bona fides of the clouds that often blanketed the sky—as on this night—with their barren oppression. Yet nothing else mattered. All interest in outside events had been discarded, as if it were the most obvious of luxuries. It was obvious that something must come sooner or later of this mass tension, but no one knew what. It was like a long thunderstorm that did not break. Apathy and exasperation were racing one another.

I followed the tramline out of the hot and odorous streets. The open space beside the Blind Institute and the Domain beyond were crowded with people in search of air. They were quiet, bivouaced for the night, but never quite still. There was no grass to sit on, only dusty earth. The Botanic Gardens were the same, ruined between the drought and the trampling people. Authority had long ago given up the thankless task of conserving them.

I no longer wanted to get to the water. These febrile cravings died easily. I was just drifting. Did it matter what I did, or where I went with those old-timers closing in ? The narrow canyons of the city offered no relief. There was nothing for the mind to feed on but nostalgia. I remembered Macquarie Place, and had a vision of it as it used to be, the three-cornered garden, the giant Port Jackson figs, dark against the pale soaring buildings, the zinnias, the cushiony buffalo grass, the statue, (I forget its original), declaiming to the street, the anchor of the Sirius on a pedestal, Macquarie's obelisk in its bear pit . . . . In the early days the officers and the higher officials lived round there. It was their compound where the children romped in safety, and in the evening the regimental band played under those same trees, lovers counted the southern stars between the leaves, and the gaiety of exiles flourished by candlelight. It was the outpost of something that had had to fall, and it might be again. It was a goal, a place with significance in a meaningless desert, a spot where we might turn at last and resist the invasion, the perishing men who came so quietly and surely through the dust. I hastened my steps like a hungry man who half remembers some forgotten fragment of food, and hurries back to ransack his belongings once more. Down I went through narrow, twisting streets, between buildings glowing with heat, but dead to light.

At first sight Macquarie Place did not seem to be greatly changed. The trees still stood, and the lights showed the dark labyrinth of their leaves scarcely breeched. It was, like all these places, crowded with people. I had the good fortune to find a seat on one of the benches. I was shaking with fatigue. All about me were points of light from cigarettes, and a murmur of talking. Those crowds had their fits of talking and their fits of silence. I turned to my neighbour and was surprised to see that he was apparently in fancy dress, white breeches, a tail coat, and a three-cornered hat. He was small and sharp, but fine too. Before I could speak to him he addressed me.

"This is nothing new, Sir, it happened before, and worse."

" Indeed ?" said I, not feeling comfortable.

" Not so much the drought—though that was bad enough, even the parrots were dropping dead out of the trees at Rose Hill—but the scarcity. You have no conception, Sir, of what it was like then."

" Was that long ago ?" I asked, trembling.,

" Some time ago. There was the same talk then of abandoning the settlement but I didn't listen to it. I hope no one listens now. Of course I've no authority these days. But if I could hang on surely you could. It was two and a half years before ships came from England that time. I'd grieve to see my work thrown away now."

I got up hurriedly. " Good-night, Captain," I said.

" Captain-General." he corrected me.

A man buttonholed me. " I've been to the Observatory every day but no one will listen to me. In the Book of Revelations. . . . ."

I broke from him. I hoisted myself on to the pedestal and leaned against the anchor. That was something solid. Two men below me were quarrelling quietly. I tried to speak to them to tell them what would be happening to all of us soon. They both fell silent.

" That's right, mate," said a man beside me, whom I had not noticed. " What we want's solidarity."

I tried to see his face. " Are you real ? " I asked.

He laughed, and called down to a friend, " Here's a poor cove gone balmy."

There was a roar of laughter, and a screech came up. " Don't laugh, you fools, repent."

I sat trembling with rage. Let it happen to them, whatever it was. I wouldn't warn them.

Two men were talking over my head.

" There's a change coming."

" I've heard that before."

" It's true this time."

" I don't hold with this metterology. It never did anything for us."

" I don't neither. I know this myself. Smell it, see ? You listen, it'll begin anytime."

" I'll wait."

" Feel that ?"

" Nope."

The country was coming to take its vengeance on the city. Climax. Apotheosis. Then nothing. Come quickly. Come quickly. All ugliness, all corruption will be burned away.

" Feel that ?"

" Something fell on my bald pate."

" Rain."

" Go on."

LISTEN

Silence fell. There was a crepitation among the leaves. Everybody stood up, stock still. I slid from the pedestal and stood with them. I felt the drops on my face. I was furious, nothing could hold me.

" No," I shouted. It couldn't come now. It was too late. Our fate was on us. We were going up in fire, consummated. It was agony to turn back now with the end we had toiled so long to reach in sight.

There were people holding me. " It isn't true," I cried. " It won't happen. No rain ever."

Someone forced me to my knees. There was a great silent ring of people around me. A match was struck and held in a cupped hand. I stared at the asphalt. Great black drops were falling on it, drying, disappearing, coming again, faster and faster, making a pattern like the leaves against the light, then coalescing and defacing itself. I stared and stared. Out on the roads, that pattern was tangling the feet of the perishing men, turning them back. Nothing would come of it now. Nothing would save us. We must take up the burden of remaking our world.

SPEAK TO ME

Since I have been sleeping badly – thin, meagre sleep like an old, shrunk blanket that never quite covers my tired mind, under which I lie, tense, cramped and unresting, or long hours without sleep at all in the *terra incognita* of the night in which nothing exists but the ticking of the clock and the whirring, concentric stillness of my own droughty brain – since I have been sleeping badly I have begun to think differently. I don't mean new thoughts but by a different process, like someone newly blind slowly fumbling out in braille an urgent message. Where there was once a barricade of healthy flesh and complacency, there is now only a membrane, fine as the membrane of the eye dividing me from thoughts as big as the sky and as old as chaos. They come like waves out of a limitless sea breaking on, but as yet not through, me. Before I had only the organized, mechanized thinking that I had been taught in my profession, my individual contribution no more than a juggling of small hard discs, like a man jingling coins in his pocket. The callow illusion of possessing my world lies behind me, dead and papery like a sloughed skin on an empty plain.

Experience bears a changed complexion now, it is no longer mechanic or inevitable in the sense that a train experiences the landscape it runs through. It is selective. Every day and every hour we are bombarded by events and incidents, few of which can register. Incident becomes experience only through a complex logic of the blood, the mind, the spirit, of things remembered and forgotten, of times and seasons. We are prisoners to ourselves and in every event is the amalgam of self. More than that there is or there strives to be a creative impact, an effort outside the law of cause and effect to force positive shape on negative event, to bring the crystal out of the magma. When it happens that the crystal is perfect, even in tragedy, the heart is comforted.

It happened today. It is Thursday and Thursday is my hospital day. I operate from 8 a.m. I operate on other days as well, of course, but Thursday is my day at the hospital where I am an honorary surgeon and the routine is always the same. The operating theatre is the least likely place for an incident, an experience, to happen. Event there is as nearly as pure as can be attained. The world for a little while is narrowed down to a circle of white light, a ritual is established, a hierarchy is imposed. The patient is not a man or a woman but a cataract, a glaucoma or whatever the trouble is. Free incident and free emotion are guarded against with as much care as infection. They are as dangerous. In a delicate manipulation there must be no break, however slight, in the concentration of attention. To import drama, as it is somewhat the fashion in plays and novels today, is nothing but cheap romanticism. But even so no situation is completely proof against the human variable.

My last patient was a boy, fifteen or sixteen years old, from the casualty ward. He had been brought in that morning from a street accident. Besides a broken collar-bone, which had already been set, he had sustained an eye injury that necessitated surgical intervention. I had before me the House surgeon's report. He had been prepared for the operation, his eyes were bandaged and I would not remove the bandage until I was ready to begin. I noticed that there was no name on his card. Evidently his people had not claimed him. It flickered through my mind, one of those thoughts that exist but are not taken up, that his injuries were hardly grave enough to explain the omission. He should have been able to speak for himself.

It was a case when the co-operation of the patient was necessary. I could not operate unless the eyeballs were in the correct position, so I had to impress on him that he must keep his eyes, under the bandage, looking downward and exercise his will so long as it would hold during the administration of the anaesthetic to keep them in that position. This can be a difficult and exasperating situation if the patient is too young or too unstable to follow a simple instruction. The operation then might have to be abandoned. I looked at the boy now, critically to judge how much co-operation I could expect and whether he was likely to panic. He was lying very still on the stretcher, his arms stiffly by his sides, his chin jutting up in a hard, an impregnable, little cliff. All the natural warm colour had drained out of his olive skin and his mouth, so eloquent when the eyes are covered, was set in pain – not so much physical pain perhaps as a deep distress, and something more that I could not at once diagnose. His pulse was good; his body, for all its slightness, well nurtured, and it was still clear that a couple of hours ago he had been full of health and vitality. The young take things so tragically. My own son . . .

I spoke to him quietly and, I hoped, reassuringly. He did not answer, nor did he show by the slightest change that he had heard me. He had not fallen asleep as patients sometimes do while they are waiting for the anaesthetic – out of fright, I think – nor was he unconscious. I spoke to him again, more loudly. There was no response. Theatre Sister, my assistant, the anaesthetist, the students, the attendants had been busied with their preparations; now, feeling that something unusual was happening, their attention slewed round us. The air stopped and waited, only the sterilizer in the corner hissed to itself. Sister raised the bandage a little over his ear. Quick as a lizard the recoil from her touch flickered over his face. I spoke to him a third time knowing it was useless. The circle drew tighter. The routine was intangibly broken by the check. You could feel them change back from the stylized personnel of the theatre to their natural selves under their trappings.

Someone was ringing down to the ward. Yes, he was conscious when he was brought in, he hadn't lost consciousness except when they gave him a whiff for his collar-bone. No, so far as Sister knew he hadn't spoken. They were rushed to death in the ward that morning. I could guess he was Sister McLeod's ideal patient.

"Shock?" my assistant suggested on a doubtful note.

The anaesthetist took the boy's pulse consideringly. He's a little, tough man with the sad, inquisitive eyes of a pug dog. He had examined the boy before and was sure in his own mind that he had missed nothing of importance. A nervous tremor followed the movements, nothing more.

"He's a deaf mute, that's what it is. There's nothing else wrong with him." He is a good anaesthetist, he can read all the minute signs and inflections of the flesh as he has need to do. "What are you going to do?" In imagination he was already packing up and getting away early.

Sister waited with that perfunctory deference they have, ready to snatch my decision the moment I opened my lips, as if it were an electric plug she was waiting to connect to the machine. The students and attendants were looking at the boy with curiosity. So that's what it was. Deaf and dumb. Poor show. But they were interested in ophthalmic surgery just now, not defects of speech and hearing.

There was a white line round the boy's lips. His distress, clamped down by his heart-breaking patience and acquiescence though it was, filled the theatre. It was easy enough now to reconstruct what had happened. There was a Deaf and Dumb School not far from the hospital. The boy had been on his way to school. They had done so much for him there and in his home – a well-cared-for child – building up his confidence, minimizing his affliction, teaching him so carefully, so triumphantly to be like other boys. This morning, because of his deafness and his confidence, this accident had happened. He was thrown out of his known world into the unknown. He was lost at once, utterly lost and forsaken and helpless. He didn't know what had happened or would happen. He was sealed in his affliction. A prisoner. He was so obviously one of us, and not one of those unfortunates set apart from life by affliction; he was so close, yet so far away behind the triple wall of his dumbness, his blindness and our stupidity. I knew that I must reach him, communicate with him, that it mattered as much to me as to him, so much that the whole fabric of our humanity even, depended on breaking through into his prison.

The anaesthetist began to pack up in a quiet way. There was a restless, pricking impatience in the room, but none of that mattered.

I took the boy's hand. I knew it so well, the sensitive hand of a delicate and afflicted child. It rested in mine like a bird shamming death. When I was a child a dumb boy lived in the same street; I'd picked up the finger language from him. It was a long time ago, twenty, thirty years, and I had forgotten it. I must remember. It was like forcing it up through my flesh as if in all those years my flesh had grown over it. I sweated under the light. I opened his hand slowly, hesitantly began to spell out on his palm the word "safe".

The boy responded at once. To say he smiled is not enough. Under the bandage his face changed, flowered. The taut lines of his body dissolved. He was released. His hands broke into fluent speech, too quick for me to follow. I held them still and began to write laboriously once more upon his palm "hospital". He was so quick to understand my difficulty, my fumbling attempts, to comprehend each word before I had half completed. It was he who was helping me, encouraging me. He let me know by small movements, of his head, of his hand, that he grasped everything I tried to say. It became easy, easier in a way than speech, less bound by convention, more eloquent and individual. The receptiveness of his hands made sense of all my groping.

I told him what was needed and what he must do. I knew that he would obey. His hand lay in mine with perfect confidence. He had not seen me or heard my voice but he trusted me. I felt the emotion that a man feels when his new-born son is laid in his arms.

I shall see him tomorrow and he will be like any other patient.

His parents will have come forward and claimed him. He will be safe in his world again. He will not need me nor shall I try to communicate with him. There are experiences that cannot be repeated.

There will be the parched, sleepless night and the unassuageable memory. My son has died a prisoner beyond help and comfort. But for one moment the crystal came clear and lay in my hand.

TREE WITHOUT EARTH

Everyone told Helen that she must make Christmas for the children's sake, or if they did not say it she could feel the pressure of their unspoken thought. They said it tenderly, urgently, secretly or with a false rallying brightness that did not deceive her. No more than Peter's steady quietness beside her did.

To Peter this Christmas was a test, a last call to someone almost out of sight and perhaps already out of hearing.

The children, not unnaturally, expected Christmas to be the same as it had always been and, digging in their short memories, like miniature archeologists unearthing a long buried city, they remembered what they had done last year and even the year before. Everything they had ever had they must have. Christmas was Christmas and nothing could change that.

Both Peter and Helen felt now a new deep awareness of their children; in her it was painful, swollen, sensitive; in him a strengthening of his sense of responsibility and of fatherhood. From different shores they saw the two small figures walking, not towards them, but upon a path of their own.

Louise was nine, burdened with her grandmother's name and gold bands on her teeth, already precociously awkward and clumsy. Helen was moved and almost frightened to see in her so soon, in the midst of her childishness, flashes of a mature understanding and, as yet barely decipherable, traces of womanliness.

Clare was just five and by a miracle had preserved her babyhood. By next Christmas that first blooming would inevitably be over but it would last for this one. Clare was too happily, squarely placed in her world, in her warm, milky health and sweet temper, to change ruthlessly in a night from baby to little girl. Everyone marvelled at Clare, but only her mother saw the budding woman in Louise.

Johnnie would have been two and this his first real Christmas.

Helen decided suddenly. Yes, they would have Christmas, a real Christmas, a tree, a party, everything. Not a children's party but one for themselves on Christmas night. They hadn't had a tree since Louise was a tiny girl, before Clare was born. Since then Helen had been too busy for the extras. Now she wasn't, she had time on her hands, one moment full, the next empty. This would be the children's first real tree. Louise had been too young for the other one and no one remembered it now. Helen saw it as a tiny illuminated spot very far away, in another world, lost, dwindling to a point of light, quenched.

Helen's decision was made so late that they were all involved in a frenzied rush. But everything could be bought, even at the last minute, if you didn't mind what you paid. Helen didn't and Peter was in no mood to cavil at bills. If only this sudden spate of energy, this Christmas fever, would break, as a thunderstorm breaks a heat wave, the cold, dark, invisible night which had lain at the heart of the home now for months, it was all he asked.

The tree could not be decorated until after Clare was in bed on Christmas eve; it was to be a surprise for her. Peter thought it should be a surprise for Louise too. He'd had a vision of himself and Helen decking the tree in the sleeping house, then going upstairs hand in hand, together again. But Helen said No, Louise could help. That would give her more pleasure than a surprise. For some reason that Peter couldn't fathom, Helen seemed to want to make up to Louise for something; what, he couldn't imagine; always to draw her, their beloved little ugly duckling, into the light. It wasn't fair to Louise, let her be a child as long as possible. She felt things far too vividly as it was. He must talk to Helen about it for the child's sake, but not now. That would be too cruel. After Christmas.

So Louise stayed up beyond her bed time and Peter brought in the tree, the sawn off top of a shapely pine, from a neighbour's garden where it had been standing in the moist soil, waiting. Only the bread crock would hold it, so the bread was dispossessed, a big red bow tied round the crock's honest neck, a bucket of water set in it and the tree shored up with bricks and stones and this engineering work finally bedded down in red tissue paper.

The tree stood silent, expectant, dark in the light, bright room. The resinous scent of its sap filled the air with a fragrance that was fresh and new but immemorially old. The waiting tree drew the household like a magnet. The neighbour who had helped to carry it in was unwilling to go though there was plenty for him to do at home; Carole came from the kitchen loath, for once, to retire into her own life. She stood awkward but eager, hoping she would be asked to help. The neighbour was politely farewelled. Helen flashed on Carole the smile which won and enslaved people.

"Aren't you meeting Harry to-night?"

"He can wait," said Carole with all the confidence of a girl who knew he would.

"Cruel girl. And on Christmas eve too."

Carole, transformed into a heartless charmer by these words, waited with diminishing hope for another minute and then clattered off.

"Peter, you'd better get on with the other decorations while Louise and I do the tree, don't you think? We'd be falling over one another if we all tried to do it, wouldn't we? And we'd be so late . . ." She put it to him charmingly and, of course, it was the sensible way to arrange the work.

Even Louise wasn't allowed to touch the tree. She could hand things, that was all. Helen worked with a withdrawn, concentrated expression, twining the red ribbon among the dark needles, hanging the stars, the bright balls, the miniature gold and silver crackers, setting the red and yellow candles on the ends of the branches, as if she followed a copy drawn deeply in her imagination.

Louise became more and more excited, jigging up and down. "This next, Mummie." "Oh Mummie, not there, *here*." "This one, this one, THIS ONE." But Helen took very little notice. She knew so well how it should go.

"Mummie, where's the fairy?"

"There isn't one, darling."

"But there was, I know there was."

"What fairy?"

"My fairy, the one on the other tree."

"But you don't remember that."

"Yes, I do. I NEVER forget ANYTHING."

She's too excited, Peter thought, she's worn out and she'll be a rag tomorrow. Helen must have been like that as a child, only pretty of course.

"WHATEVER will we do without a fairy? What happened to it?"

"Clare played with it when she was tiny and broke it."

Louise couldn't remember that. "Couldn't we get another fairy?"

"No, darling, we don't want a fairy."

"Yes, we do."

"We can imagine it."

"Can you?"

"Yes, so can you. Look, I'll put the big silver star on top."

"Oh Mummie, not the SILVER star, the GOLD one."

"I think it ought to be silver."

"No no no." Louise had burst into tears.

Helen dropped everything and ran to her. "Yes, darling, of course, the gold star. And look, the tree's finished and you must go to bed. Mummie will put you to bed."

She took Louise by the hand and led her, now docile with hanging head and gulping on every second step, up the stairs. She looked down at Peter, shaking her head in self accusation and asking his forgiveness with her eyes.

Very gently she undressed the little girl and smiling tenderly washed the tear stains from her face. "Nothing to cry about, Lulu, we have a lovely, lovely tree, haven't we, darling?"

Everyone knew that Lulu was a frightful, terrible name for a girl to have but it could be used secretly between them.

"Yes, Mummie."

Thin arms shot round her neck in fierce protective love. Lulu had let herself be undressed like a baby to please her. She gathered the child as fiercely into her own arms in the first passionate embrace. They were no longer mother and child but mother and daughter.

The moment was over. Louise relaxed, and with closed eyes nuzzled against her mother. Helen laid her down on the bed and drew the sheet up to her chin. "Happy Christmas, Lulu."

Peter fidgeted downstairs, uneasy, waiting to know where Helen wanted the holly wreath, waiting. Helen came down the stairs. She looked serene. "She's sleeping", she said and went back to the tree.

It seemed to be finished but she still worked on it, adding a touch here and there, all of them right. The look of concentration was back on her face. When Peter came to admire her work, he felt that she invisibly shouldered him away.

Without a word Helen went upstairs and came back with something bright in her hand. It was a necklace he had given her when Johnnie was born. She twisted it along a branch and let it drip down half seen.

She said in a matter-of-fact tone, "It wanted something just there and that's exactly right. Don't you think so? The tree is ready now."

Didn't she remember? Her voice and manner suggested that she didn't. But she couldn't possibly forget. His mind was confused. Was this tree more than a tree, was the hanging of a necklace an atavistic rite? Something deeper and older than either he or she could understand?

Helen was looking at the tree impartially and critically as if she were assessing her work. "It is nice, don't you think?"

It was lovely, in all its decorations, rich but light and gay. It was the Burning Bush, it was the Feast of Wan. He couldn't speak. Had something happened? Had she found a way at last out of the pain and grieving and silence? Was the hard core mystically resolved? He dared not look at her.

But Helen didn't seem to want to know what he was thinking. She was already going upstairs. She paused and smiled at him, the smile that won people and enslaved them.

"I'm tired now, darling. Would you be an angel, do the locking up and bring me up just a tiny drink?"

They were as far apart as ever.

The night was a narrow dark canyon between the days. At the bottom of it there was a thin trickle of sleep. When Peter woke in the first light Helen was already awake, staring towards the window, haggard and worn in the thin light. He wondered if she were going to get through the big day. He felt all their elaborate preparations, the decorations, the tree, piled suddenly into his arms like funeral wreaths. The old feeling of despair, of being able to do nothing for her, nothing, was back in its place. He had tried too often. When he'd said, oh fatuously, and probably not for the first time either, "I'm still here, darling, we have one another" she had turned on him in the ferocity of her grief. "Why couldn't it have been you instead, or me?" She'd hardly known what she was saying but it had come from somewhere just the same. Here was Christmas morning, and if he couldn't say "Happy Christmas" what was there to say?

Now had come the most difficult moment of all, the moment that struck at his heart with an almost unbearable sense of loss. For now Johnnie, the early riser, the joyful, the uninhibited, would have come running in to wake them. The moment was not to be shared for Helen would not share. She had shut herself from him in her hoarded grief, but surely not for ever. If it were almost unbearable for him, might it not be quite unbearable for her? Would she not shiver like some frail, brittle glass vessel on some such moment as this? Fear ran like cold water in his veins. How could he ever explain to Helen the bleak reasoning that saved his own sanity and supported him while it did not comfort? This was the knowledge that to lose, to suffer, to die were as much a part of living, as natural, as birth and happiness. Men and women took on the human lot and when it could not be changed stood by it for the dignity and integrity of their souls. Peter had never sought after reasons or been a philosopher but now in his need something like a philosophy had risen out of himself. But he could not impart it. It lay dumbly within him.

Clare ran in dragging her full pillow case. "Merry Christmas Mummie. Merry Christmas Daddie." Louise was behind her with her pillow case, a little diffident because she knew the truth about Santa Claus now ("I'll tell her, no one else shall.") and was unsure of her new rôle. But there was no trace left of last night's emotion and strain.

Helen was sitting up, laughing, holding out her arms. "Come in, darlings. Merry Christmas. Merry Christmas. Here you are Clare, get up on the bed and Louise on Daddie's bed. Let's see what you have there."

Treasure after treasure emerged from the pillow cases. Helen had been lavish. Clare, her cheeks scarlet, ran from one to the other afraid of missing something, too excited to open her own parcels. Louise shone with happiness. When Carole brought in tea they wouldn't let her go. She had to sit down on the floor and share it all.

The father looked at the mother. She's wonderful, he thought, she's marvellous. With so much courage everything is sure to come right – how could I ever have doubted her?

Helen whispered at last, "We can't hurry them but there really is a lot to be done . . ."

She had orchestrated the day and now she must conduct it. First the flowers, all the neighbours were stripping their gardens for her. She had so many she hardly knew what to do with them and every spare basin, jug and saucepan was cunningly converted to a vase. The decorations which had looked artificial last night were filled out and brought to life with flowers. The rooms were a work of art, everyone said so. Helen had the gift.

Only when the flowers were done did they open the door and let Clare in to see the tree. She ran and stopped. It was almost too much and there were too many people watching her, but when they encouraged her she looked at everything and was excited and happy just as they wanted her to be.

"Daddie" she said, pointing at the stars, the candles, the ribbons, "are those Johnnie's presents?"

"No darling," he answered, keeping his voice very even, "they belong to us all."

Clare often talked about Johnnie but Louise never did, never, and she was likely to be angry with Clare and slap her. Nothing like that happened to-day.

Then there was the arrival of the aunts and uncles and dinner which was a very handsome meal, and after dinner the children had to lie down and rest but could take just one Christmas present each in to bed with them. It took so long to choose which that there was hardly any time for lying down. The mother encouraged as many uncles and aunts as possible to lie down too for she had to begin immediately after dinner to prepare the evening's party.

When Helen went up to dress it was late but everything was ready. She heard people arrive but that didn't hurry her. Peter was there to welcome them and give them drinks and Louise, grave and important, was quite prepared to show any lady, who brought a coat this warm night, where to put it.

Helen dressed with great care in a long grey silk dress with a wine coloured sash and shoulder knot. It was a long time since she had dressed like this and she seemed to feel her body unfolding like a tight bud softly opening to warmth, as she tended it. At last she was ready. They would be thinking that she was not going to appear, even Peter would be getting anxious, wondering if he should pop up to see if anything had happened to her. For a long time now he had kept that careful, anxious, infuriating vigil.

At first no one saw her on the stairs, then Clare called shrilly "Mummie" and everyone looked. They surged towards her and those who held wine glasses raised them in a toast. She saw a blaze of light and colour, Peter's face, adoring. Other men's eyes. She took the party as a swimmer the water, it carried her, buoyant. Her nerves as taut as the strings of a harp responded to every breath but they gave out a sigh of music instead of pain. Her mind, transparent with fatigue and stimulated by it, yielded a new sharp awareness. She knew what everyone thought. Some "How could she?", others "How brave!", "How beautiful!", "It's for the children" "For Peter". A few that they did not like it at all, just a few.

It was the right sort of party, not wild, for this was Christmas night, but effulgent. Only the tree stood aloof, magical. The tree is my partner to-night, thought Helen. The necklace sparkled and was just exactly right in the place where it hung. Talk and laughter filled the room. Peter relaxed. All was well.

"Where's Clare?" someone asked and they found her asleep in a corner as naturally as a puppy sleeps. A little indulgent laugh ran round the room but when Peter lifted her up and stood for a moment with her in his arms there was silence for the memory of the dead child was drawn slowly, like a barb, over every heart.

Helen whispered to Louise, "Go too and help Daddie put Clare to bed. It's getting late." She watched Peter and the children till the bend of the stairs hid them. "He's good to them," she thought, "and better for them than I am, even for Louise."

The incident had changed the quality of the party, it had grown quiet as if the still warm night had stepped in through the windows to be one of the company. It was too early to go home yet the party was ended. Someone suggested that they sing carols. A strong voice began "Silent night, holy night" and others joined in, steadying themselves on the selfless swell of the air. Beautiful and poignant beyond all reason they finished it because they had begun it. Helen stood like one frozen. In everyone there was now a longing to go home, to be in their own places on Christmas night. A guest with more initiative than the others, pleaded an excuse and said goodbye. The others followed quickly. Helen gave each her cold hand in parting and without waiting, or looking back or smiling, walked up the stairs.

In her room she began automatically to undress. A black wave of grief towered ready to engulf her. Christmas was over, tomorrow would begin again the succession of days that were all alike. Let the wave swallow her, she would still carry something precious with her, something she would never share. From the back of a drawer she brought out a phial of sleeping tablets. Her face as intent as a sleep walker's, she cascaded them into her hand. she would be asleep before Peter came up. It was all she asked for, a little sleep.

Downstairs among the dying flowers the wavering candles and the broken food the immaculate tree kept its vigil.

ONE BRIGHT LEAF

Our Father was a capable man, more than that, he had ideas, he could see opportunities even if he could not take them. He could have been anything, an engineer, a scientist perhaps, an inventor, a public figure . . . but there was the farm, a few stony acres. He was an only son. From childhood the farm needed him and he had a duty to it for his parents' sake. When they died he inherited it. He was already married and I, at least, had been born. So he could not leave the farm. It was security of a sort, and our Mother had been born on just such a farm. She had all the skills, the caring for animals, the spinning, the weaving, the making and the doing, so that hardly anything had to be bought. No other life would have suited her – only a bigger, better farm with a hundred sheep instead of ten. She had her creativeness, our Father had his. There were six children. I was the eldest, then the twins, Olaf and Laurans, the two girls, Ana and Kristen, and Bjorn. Many mouths, but a work force too.

Children know little of their parents' secret lives. I do not know yet how strong and deep was the bond that held them to one another, only that there was a bond. I came to know that our Mother was a passionate woman with an iron self control. She ruled us, but was always just. She was neither affectionate nor heartless. Her praise, when and if it came, was above rubies. She could laugh too. I was nearer to our Father than to our Mother.

Every year when things were slack on the farm our Father went up into the mountains to cut slates. It helped out. When I was eleven he took me with him. It was hard work. On the first evening when we made camp, he suddenly asked me to show him my hands. They were torn and bleeding. I had not complained or cried. He was proud of me but blamed himself. He brought mutton fat, and the strips of linen he kept for cuts, and bound up my hands. As he bent over me in the light of the lantern I saw the tenderness in his face and felt the gentleness of his hands. He would only let me do a little cutting each day till I toughened up. Each year after that I went with him; he did not take the others.

It was like a holiday. I learned about stillness and the stars. It was only a small outcrop of slate, no one else worked it, it was too far from anywhere. After we had left, a cart came up the other side of the mountain, where there was a better road, collected the slates and our Father was paid.

We had to climb through the pine forest on our side and when we came out of the wood on to the windy top we were there. The trees haunted me and I was glad to be above them tho' I was always conscious that they encircled us, dark, secret, dour. They were watchful and unchanging, evergreen without gaiety. Oddly, I felt myself their prisoner. Perhaps our Father felt the same.

One of his ideas, an opportunity he was able to seize, was to buy for very little a derelict bus. He saw that it could help out and it interested him to make something out of what was nearly nothing. He was clever with engines and he got this one to go. The body was mended and painted. We all helped. That bus became another member of the family.

Our Father saw an opening in transport. In the region there was a glacier, not much of a one, but still a glacier, and tourists in the season came to see it if they could walk the distance. There was a rough road, a right-of-way across farmlands, including ours. When the tourist season was over, supplies could be brought in the bus. I was the driver, and, as there were so many gates to be opened and shut, I took one of the boys with me. It was usually Bjorn. The twins were too canny to let themselves in for a job like that. They wanted to do everything together.

We thought the tourists very odd, so foreign that they made no impact on our lives. They talked a lot and asked silly questions, like "Are there any trolls about here? My, what a talking point that would be." We picked up a bit of American from them but did not have to understand all we heard.

Bjorn stood behind the driving seat holding on, ready to jump out and open a gate. I could see his face in the mirror, absorbed in my driving the bus. The passengers chattered "like a cage full of parrots", I thought, though I'd never seen a parrot. There are none in the pine forests. Often the women made a pass at Bjorn, they wanted to pat him, to give him something, a wrapped sweet, a kiss, even money. Our Father would never have allowed that. Bjorn put his hands behind his back and, shaking his head, gave them his shy, sweet smile, giving no offence. He would have been twelve years old, nearly thirteen.

He liked our bus rides best in the autumn and early winter before the roads were snow-bound, when there were no tourists and we often had to put the lights on coming home.

I drove faster, scudding over the rough road. Bjorn's exhilaration breathed on the back of my neck.

There was one day in autumn, very still, promising nothing except the coming winter. The early dark was beginning to gather and I was anxious to get on because we had a cargo of winter supplies to be delivered round the district. I wasn't looking for passengers. It was Bjorn who told me we were being hailed. I stopped of course. There were three people at the roadside, two men and a woman. They were foreigners, which was very strange at that time and at that place, miles from habitation. If there were any foreigners about, out of season, the news generally went around like wild-fire. No rumours had reached me. I turned on all the lights in the bus. These were not tourists, they were finely dressed, the men had an air of command. I don't know how I recognised it, but I did. And the woman, the woman was beautiful. I had never seen a beautiful woman before. My sisters are comely but this was different. She was tall and slender with dark clustering hair and her eyes – I'm no good at describing women's faces – her eyes were luminous, they devoured her face, they asked, but I don't know what they asked. It flashed across my mind that she might be the prisoner of the two men and I should do something about it. I could not do anything, I could not ask questions.

One man spoke Norwegian with a foreign accent I could not place. He named the place he wanted to go to, about three miles away, and paid the fares.

We drove on and I looked at Bjorn. He had moved a step forward facing the strangers with one tense hand still holding the back of my seat. I could see the woman in the mirror and she was looking at Bjorn, a little smile lifted her lips and shone in her eyes. There was recognition. They came from different worlds, they were a thousand miles apart but each saw the beauty of the other, one perhaps asking for escape into the safe world of a child, the other asking to be let into life.

We drove on. We came to the appointed place and stopped. Bjorn let go of my seat and moved forward. One man stepped out of the bus and held out his hand to the woman. With a quick movement she folded Bjorn in her arms and kissed him. Then she left the bus and the other man followed her. The place was nowhere. It did have a name, but nothing else except the trees.

Bjorn stood behind me holding on. I saw his face in the mirror. It was transfigured.

We completed the journey, delivered the goods and went home. I knew Bjorn did not want me to tell what had happened and I would not. In a way it had happened to me too. I had seen beauty and recognised it in Bjorn.

I kept the money the man had given me for the fares and substituted my own money for it. While I had it hidden away I could look at it and know that I was not imagining something. It had really happened.

Time flowed on. Bjorn and I never spoke of that autumn evening. No rumour of strangers in the district ever surfaced.

When the war came and Norway was involved Olaf and Laurans enlisted. They went into the mine sweepers. The house was much quieter. In a few months Bjorn would be old enough to be called up and it would be quieter still. The authorities did not want me because of my foot. It was just as well because I was needed on the farm. It has never gone against me. Ever since I was a boy I've done the work of two men and more. The country needed its farmers to wring the utmost from the soil.

We had bad news, the pastor brought it. The boys' ship had been blown up and they were posted missing. He begged us not to despair, missing did not mean lost. They were fine, strong boys and could swim. It would be some time before it could be cleared up in the chaos of war. They were as likely to survive as any of the crew, they could reach the shore in some wild, out of the way place or be picked up by another ship bound for a distant port.

Our Mother was very brave and held us together. We must put our trust in God and carry on. First we must eat our evening meal. It would be no help to anyone if we didn't. She even put on a cheerful face but I saw her looking at Bjorn.

At the end of the meal Kristen brought the Bible to our Mother as usual and she read aloud from the Book of Psalms. To me it seemed all very far away from our world and I was not comforted. Then she asked us to pray for our brothers. We bent our heads and prayed silently, or seemed to; I could not. It was our Father's lips that I saw quivering.

Olaf did come back months later. He had an incredible story of survival that he did not want to tell, a saga. He was changed and not only physically. He was emaciated and ill from privation but it went deeper. It was almost as if he had a sense of guilt because he lived and Laurans died. He was invalided out of the service but did eventually recover his health and strength. He was young. His home-coming lacked joy, he felt none, he was too exhausted and Bjorn was already in the war. The action was on the sea so that was where Bjorn went too.

We were just sitting down to the evening meal when we saw the black figure of the pastor toiling up the hill. We knew it was no pastoral visit. He had a telephone and none of the crofters had, so he had taken on the burden of bringing the news, good or bad. Mostly bad. We knew. He tried to say the right things but there were no right things. He looked at our Mother and the only consolation he had to offer withered on his lips. Our Father thanked him for his intention and he went away.

This time there was no hope, she had no care for us. It was her grief. Her face was a mask of stony anguish and I thought: "She could die of grief." But she could not. Ana, I realised, was her Mother over again. She too was turned to stone but not such hard stone. Olaf was an onlooker. So, in a way, was I. He was beyond feeling; I had work here and now.

Kristen carried away the uneaten meal and stood hesitating. And then she brought the Bible and put it in front of our Mother, thinking perhaps she was offering comfort. Our Mother rose in fury and picking up the Bible put it back on the shelf.

Then Kristen broke and ran away weeping into the next room. Our Father followed her and, big girl that she was, took her onto his lap and cradled her. In the light that fell in there I could see the silver streaks on his cheek.

Bjorn was dead and now we knew that he was the one our Mother loved.

Our Mother and Father died years ago, within a few days of one another, the girls are married, Olaf has gone to sea. I might see him once in a year, the difference is still there.

I live alone. I have the farm. What else is there?

I think of Bjorn. He had his moment. At least *he* had something.

VIRAGO MODERN CLASSICS

The first Virago Modern Classic, *Frost in May* by Antonia White, was published in 1978. It launched a list dedicated to the celebration of women writers and to the rediscovery and reprinting of their works. Its aim was, and is, to demonstrate the existence of a female tradition in fiction which is both enriching and enjoyable. The Leavisite notion of the 'Great Tradition', and the narrow, academic definition of a 'classic', has meant the neglect of a large number of interesting secondary works of fiction. In calling the series 'Modern Classics' we do not necessarily mean 'great' — although this is often the case. Published with new critical and biographical introductions, books are chosen for many reasons: sometimes for their importance in literary history; sometimes because they illuminate particular aspects of womens' lives, both personal and public. They may be classics of comedy or storytelling; their interest can be historical, feminist, political or literary.

Initially the Virago Modern Classics concentrated on English novels and short stories published in the early decades of this century. As the series has grown it has broadened to include works of fiction from different centuries, different countries, cultures and literary traditions. In 1984 the Victorian Classics were launched; there are separate lists of Irish, Scottish, European, American, Australian and other English speaking countries; there are books written by Black women, by Catholic and Jewish women, and a few relevant novels by men. There is, too, a companion series of Non-Fiction Classics constituting biography, autobiography, travel, journalism, essays, poetry, letters and diaries.

By the end of 1986 over 250 titles will have been published in these two series, many of which have been suggested by our readers.

TOMORROW AND TOMORROW AND TOMORROW

By M. Barnard Eldershaw

New Introduction by Anne Chisholm

Set in Australia of the past and the future, this remarkable work is two novels in one.

It is the twenty-fourth century. Knarf, a writer, lives in a society of technocratic socialism that has abolished war and poverty through "scientific" laws. Knarf has written a novel which begins in November 1924 and tells the story of an Australian working man, Harry Munster, of his hopes, fears and loves, of his family, their friends and lovers. Through their eyes we experience the terrible years of the Depression: years of rising anger that culminate, at the end of the Second World War, in civil disturbance and the threat of a Third World War. When first published in 1947 these stirring passages were seriously cut by the Government censor: now for the first time the full uncensored text is printed as the authors wrote it. The result is both a warm and vivid portrait of one man and his times, and a prophetic vision of what was to follow – the nuclear shadow which is our common inheritance.

Australian Virago Modern Classics

Also of interest

PHYLLIS SHAND ALLFREY
The Orchid House

SYLVIA ASHTON-WARNER
Spinster

MARGARET ATWOOD
Bodily Harm
Dancing Girls

The Edible Woman
Lady Oracle
Life Before Man
Surfacing

ELIOT BLISS
Luminous Isle

NADINE GORDIMER
The Lying Days
Occasion for Loving

KATHERINE MANSFIELD
The Aloe